For Mum...
Your faith in me is my strength.
Thank you for believing.

THE OTHER SIDE
of the
LOOKING GLASS

Kathleen Harryman

www.kathleenharryman.com

ISBN: 978-1-64970-572-3
Second Edition published by Kathleen Harryman
July 2020

Editing, Cover Design and Formatting by The Book Khaleesi
www.thebookkhaleesi.com
June, 2020

Books by Kathleen Harryman

THRILLER:
THE OTHER SIDE OF THE LOOKING GLASS
WHEN DARKNESS FALLS
HIDDEN DANGER

HISTORICAL ROMANCE:
THE PROMISE

POETRY:
LIFE'S ECHOES

COMING IN 2020...

PARANORMAL YOUNG ADULT ROMANCE:
VAMPWITCH SERIES:
BOOK ONE: HUNTED

PARANORMAL ROMANCE:
ANGELS AT WAR TRILOGY:
BOOK ONE: THE BLACK FEATHER

Acknowledgments

The Other Side of the Looking Glass is my debut novel. Writing a novel is something I have dreamt of since I was able to read. My parents always read to me as a child, and it is them I must thank for first planting this small seed of magic within me.

I could never have achieved what I have without the love, help and support of my family. I love you all and thank you for being the sparkle in my life.

It is nice to have the chance to revisit my first novel, and I hope this latest edition shines more than the previous edition. The main story stays the same, however, there are many tweaks that I feel improves upon the original, which has received some outstanding book reviews.

To those readers who have taken the time to read and write a book review, I would like to thank you. Your encouragement is inspirational.

As such, I would like to acknowledge and pay tribute to all readers out there. Without you, a story would never have the chance to flourish, and it will forever remain hidden. Thank you for reading and breathing life into the story. An author is nothing without you.

I would like to thank Eeva Lancaster for her superb editing skills, and all the wonderful fairy folk at The Book Khaleesi --- Eeva, Robert and Samantha --- you really are magical beings.

Chapter One

KATE

The clinical smell of detergent penetrates my senses and my eyes flutter open. I find myself staring at a white-tiled commercial ceiling, questioning if I am awake or asleep – though it does seem like a rather strange dream to have. I blink. The ceiling remains. My senses give my brain a nudge and it fires up but provides no answers. Brows wrinkling in confusion, I begin trying to determine what is going on.

One thing I am certain of, is that my body is sore and stiff. Muscles aching, I remain as I am, twisting my head to the right. The sun glares through a wide, steel window. From the sun's height in the sky, I estimate it has been there some time.

A feeling of guilt settles over me. It appears sleeping in isn't something I indulge in.

To my right, between the bed and window, is a small white cupboard and a plastic-coated armchair. Sunflowers sit in a vase on the bedside cupboard. I like sunflowers. Though at this moment, I fail to recall why.

An irritating beep-beep sound comes from my left, and I swing my eyes in that direction, lifting my head slightly. Wires litter my body and a pink cellular hospital blanket covers me. The beeping begins to make sense, along with the plastic-coated chair and wires. I am in a hospital.

A sigh escapes my lips as I resist the urge to panic. Instead, I acknowledge my dislike of hospitals. Then again, name a patient or visitor who *likes* them. There is that clinical smell that lingers long after you have left, and they are full of sick people. At present, I am reluctant to place myself in the *'sick people'* category, even if my brain is screaming at me, telling me I wouldn't be here if I was fit and well.

Tentatively, I sniff the air. This hospital does smell nicer than the ones I have stayed in and visited before. At present, I am unable to *remember* ever spending time in or visiting a hospital, though I'm sure I have done so.

My eyes widen and adrenalin is released into my bloodstream. Hands shaking, my breathing quickens. Panic grips me. *Why can't I remember anything?* My eyes fly round the room, unseeing. *What has happened to me?*

If I am in a hospital, I am safe and cared for. Quantifying this fact allows reason to be heard. Though my heart still hammers, its beat is more regular than it was. My memories are in there, somewhere, I just need to find them. It's probably the drugs they have given me, clouding and confusing my brain.

Closing my eyes, I demand that my brain starts its cognitive processing. My demand falls into a black hole of nothingness. Not giving up, I decide to think about the sunflowers, as they'd triggered a feeling of happiness. Unfortunately, this simple request is met with vacuity, and a hollow feeling takes up residence in the pit of my stomach. The only mental input I receive is that sunflowers are bright, cheery plants.

My eyes fly open and I face the frightening fact that my life is a blank.

This notion sends my pulse hammering and a nauseous feeling erupts inside me. Cold sweat lines my skin and my hands begin to tremble. Reason's voice tells me there is nothing I can do about my loss of memory. It is temporary, caused by whatever event resulted in my being in the hospital. Scaring myself isn't going to help. I force my body to relax, taking deep, even breaths.

Time drifts as I concentrate on my breathing. When I feel in control of my emotions, I start to wonder about myself. *What do I look like? What colour are my eyes? Age?* This line of self-questioning is easier to rectify than trying to remember my whole life story.

Lifting my hands in front of my eyes, I stare at them for answers.

I am not a child, or a teenager, or even a young woman. Thirty-something, perhaps. There is a sense that this age *fits.* I tick off the question surrounding my age. My hands also tell me the colour of my skin, which is a rich, light brown. Not a tan. This is my natural skin tone.

I go through what I have learnt about myself so far. I am around thirty, and of non-white descent. Once again, I wonder about the colour of my eyes. A tiny buzz of excitement zips through me. I need a mirror. My fingers drum with impatience as I look around my clinical environment. There is no mirror within reach.

As it is hard to view eye colour lying in bed, I move my legs to the edge of the mattress. There is a heaviness in my limbs that I hadn't noticed before. Like wading through quicksand rather than bedlinen.

Something touches my skin and I stop moving, eyebrows raising in question as I wonder what it could be. My requirement for a mirror is side-tracked by the discovery that there is something between my legs that doesn't belong. Lifting the sheets, I look down into the semi darkness. The shadows allow for little visibility. My arms are heavy and start shaking as I try to push myself into a sitting position. Sweat coats my skin again and I feel like I have run a marathon. *Argh!* My arms give out and I flop onto the pillows.

Staring at the ceiling tiles, I notice a small stain from an old water leak. The shape comes in and out of focus as I work out my next move. One thing I become conscious of is that finding out what I look like has moved to the top of my *most-important-things-to-do-today* list.

Fingers drumming on the cotton blanket, I work at finding a solution to my current problem.

Ping! It comes to me. Hospital beds have switches to raise the patient to a sitting position. My fingers move, seeking out the control box. It takes a while, as some thoughtful person has hung it on the frame above my head. That I hadn't noticed it before amazes me. My mind has been busy, and my eyes with it. I reach for the controls. It takes me some time to work out what button does what, but once I do, I click down, and the bed moves. Impatience crawls at my skin at the slow mechanical motion. Once in position, I raise the cotton blanket. A pale-pink tube coils between my legs. I follow it as it disappears to my right. Stunned, I take another look. The tube remains. *What on earth is a tube doing there?*

I see this as a minor setback on my journey to self-discovery, but one that needs investigating further. The tube comes out from beneath the blankets, down the right side of the bed, where a bag of urine sits. My head falls back onto the pillows and, as my angle has now changed, I find myself staring at a dark-pink door rather than the stain on the ceiling.

It is clear that I have been here for some time, otherwise there would be no need for a catheter. There also appears to be no expectation I am going to bounce out of bed soon. *Just what happened to me?*

A dull throb pounds in my head and I lift my right hand, massaging my temple. A needle sticks out of my left hand, and my headache amplifies. Soreness tugs beneath the skin of my hand.

There are two things I find upsetting. One – when I compare my right hand to my left, I notice that my left hand is twice the size of my right. I am positive I was not born with this deformity. I link the increase in size to the needle stuck in it. Two – a bandage is wrapped around my head.

Again, I question what happened to me.

This thought rattles round my brain for some time. Given my present predicament, there is nothing I can do but wait for someone to check on me. My brain isn't complying to my requests for clarity and the door to my memory is still sealed shut.

To pass the time and to stop myself from getting frustrated, I look about the room from my sitting position. The colour scheme is pink, from light to dark. Besides the door in front of the bed, there is one on my left. I make the assumption that one leads to the bathroom, the other to freedom. While the room meets my basic needs, it lacks any personal touches, other than a picture of a patch of grass with daisies. From my lack of appreciation for the painting, it is clear I am not into art.

Being in a room on my own, there is nothing to steer my

attention from my current predicament. Though, as hospitals go, this is a nice place. I must have money.

Though my head hurts and my left hand is sore, I can find no reason why I would be in a room on my own. My injuries aren't life-threatening.

The door to the room opens and a nurse walks in. She makes her way to the foot of the bed. Her attention is taken up by the metal clipboard, and she doesn't notice I am awake.

"Do you have a mirror?"

The nurse jumps and I try to hide my smile.

Her pink hair sits on top of her head in a skewwhiff top-knot. Some of the pins have loosened their grip and are hanging on to stray wisps of hair. From the lines around her eyes and the darkening patches under them, she is probably entering the last few hours of her shift. Her pale-blue dress falls above her knees, hugging her stomach and hips a little too tightly.

"You're awake."

I present her with a tight-lipped smile, wondering if my request for a mirror has fallen on deaf ears.

"I'll go get the doctor."

And with that, she is gone, and I am alone again, without a mirror.

My fingers beat against the blanket as my annoyance builds. While I understand the nurse's primary concern is my health, she didn't assist me in uncovering the truth about myself. There's a part of me that acknowledges I am being one of those *awful patients* nurses often speak about. I refuse to accept full responsibility.

I am unable to coax my mind away from obsessing over a mirror. I am haunted by the need to look at my reflection and to have the door to my memories open. To see recognition, or not. That is the scary part. How am I going to feel if the person in the mirror is nothing but a stranger? I refuse to allow myself to give in to these thoughts. I turn my mind to another problem. My left hand.

Laying both my right and left together, I re-examine the difference in size. With gentle fingers, I touch the surface of my left hand. Pain explodes and I quickly remove my fingers from the sensitive spot.

My impatience with the nurse grows as my problems mount. Time is going by at a torturous rate, and I wonder if the nurse has boarded a plane due to the lack of doctors in England.

How do I know I'm in England? I glance at the rain now beating against the window. That alone is a clear indicator. It always rains in England.

As I seem to like making lists, I comprise a mental inventory of all the things that are bothering me at present.

1. Lack of mirror.
2. The size of my left hand.
3. Memory loss.
4. Where has the nurse gone…?

The door opens, preventing me from adding anything further. A man in a white coat walks in, followed by the wayward nurse. His lips are turned up and his expression is one of delight. His patient is awake, and that has to be good news for us all. His warm, brown eyes sweep over me as he makes a quick visual assessment before approaching the bed and looking at the chart on the metal clipboard.

There are no lines pulling at the corners of his eyes, and he radiates pleasantness and energy. His face is clean shaven, and I make the assumption he is just starting his shift. He reminds me of George Clooney. It is strange, the things I can remember. Whilst George Clooney is as gorgeous today as he was back in his *ER* days, I would prefer to remember more about me, not him.

The doctor's black trousers sit at half-mast. Given his age, I doubt they're too short because he's outgrown them. Maybe he washed them on a hot cycle in error. I have had my fair share of laundry disasters. Whoa... Hang on... Memory flash...

And that's it. Not helpful.

Perhaps my earlier assumption of being rich is wishful thinking. If I have money, I wouldn't have to do my own washing. Unless I have just inherited it.

The doctor towers over the nurse by a good foot. The fact that she's on the short side only makes him look taller, and he dwarfs her already-small frame.

"It's good to see you awake, Mrs. Thornton." His voice is deep, his words nicely pronounced, and I am surprised to find his deep twang appealing.

Mrs. Thornton? The name doesn't sound familiar, but – as there is only one patient in the room – the likelihood that he's referring to someone else is limited. My headache is getting worse due to the constant questions rattling round it. I latch on to my previous request for a mirror, if only to give my brain something else to focus on.

"Do you have a mirror?"

The doctor's eyebrows shoot up. My question has surprised him. He recovers fast and turns to the nurse. "Would you get Mrs. Thornton a mirror, please?"

She gives the doctor an adoring look before walking out the door.

"I'm Dr. Jonas. I've been looking after you since you arrived two days ago."

We do not shake hands.

"Two days!" I gasp.

The fact that I have been unconscious for two days is unsettling, and my heart responds in kind, its beat picking up. Shock washes over me and the muscles in my jaw pulsate. Fingers entwining around the cotton blanket, I am mindful of my rising nervousness. With deep intakes of breath, I try to calm the fear which has nibbled away at my mind since I woke up.

The lack of a wedding band on my left hand explains why it never occurred to me that I am married. Of course, there is the possibility that I am divorced, or even widowed, which would explain the 'Mrs.' without the ring.

While my brain whirs away, Dr. Jonas is busy checking my vitals. He's nodding, which I take as a good sign. The nurse's continued absence makes me wonder if she is back on the same plane she boarded to get the doctor. It seems to be taking her an abnormal amount of time to locate a mirror, and I am in need of the distraction.

The door opens and I sigh in relief.

Dr. Jonas has finished giving me the once-over, and as soon as I have the mirror, I will ask him if he can arrange for the catheter bag to be removed as well as the needle from my hand. My lack of energy is not going to stop me from using a toilet.

I look past the doctor, my hands outstretched, ready to receive the mirror, only it's not the nurse entering the room. A man in a well-cut dark-grey suit strides purposefully over to my bed. I watch his steps hesitate as he sees I am awake. A strange expression crosses his face. It makes me uneasy. He becomes aware that I am watching him. A smile forms and his eyes widen in surprise. I think the emotion he is trying for is 'joy'. His eyes fail to fill with pretend warmth, and my unease turns to suspicion.

Like a fruit bat spying a grape, he races over to me.

Incapable of any quick action, I hope the metal bed can take the force of him hitting it. Though he isn't a large man, and I would be hard-pressed to find any muscle beneath the expensive suit, his growing speed alone gives him mass.

Had I been able to, I would have leaped off the bed and shut myself in the bathroom. Or, better still, run out the door to freedom. As it is, I have no alternative but to brace myself for impact. Given that there is a doctor present I feel, perhaps mistakenly, I will be OK.

As the stranger pins me to his chest, he catches the needle in my left hand. I cry out as pain explodes. This doesn't alter the man's grip on me, and I worry that I am going to be suffocated by Armani. My hope that I'll die uneventfully in my sleep from old age, is slipping away from me. I press my right hand against his chest to push him off.

"Mr. Thornton! Mr. Thornton!" Dr. Jonas is yelling, and I am acutely aware I share the same surname as the strange man.

Dear lord, please don't say this is my husband.

The doctor places a hand on Mr. Thornton's arm, moving him off of me. Not far enough for my liking, but at least I can breathe.

The small distance allows me a better view of the man I'm hoping isn't my husband. 'Thornton' isn't an uncommon surname.

The stranger is clean shaven. His features chiselled, giving him a hawk-like appearance, and his eyes are shifty. At just under six foot, the man is of average height. No flame of remembrance ignites, and I don't feel a spark of attraction towards him. It is impossible for me to think I would marry this man.

"Sorry." His apology lacks conviction.

Mr. Thornton is well spoken, and his voice suggests that he is a well-educated man. He is a man used to getting his own way. I find myself disliking him without a reason. But instinct is all I have right now, and it's telling me this man is *trouble*, and not the enjoyable kind.

If we are married, are we getting a divorce? Perhaps I married him while inebriated, before the alcohol had a chance to wear off. It would make sense. I try and imagine myself so drunk I would marry the man in the posh suit. Nope, not happening.

My head hits the pillow and I stare at the pink door in front of me. Mr. Thornton continues to hover at my side. I can feel his displeasure. My silence isn't helping the situation.

Avoiding the stranger, I raise my left hand. "My hand hurts, and it's all swollen."

Both Dr. Jonas and Mr. Thornton look down at my hand. I raise my right one so they can see the size difference.

"Doctor?" It is strange how some people can make one word sound like a scolding. Mr. Thornton possesses the knack.

Dr. Jonas reacts to the clipped demand of the well-dressed stranger and begins removing the needle.

Mr. Thornton is a man of means. He smells of money, and lots of it. He oozes the stuff, right down to the stitching on his expensive suit, and the glint of his Sky-Dweller oyster and 18ct Everose gold Rolex watch. I remain unimpressed. At least I'm not shallow.

"Do you think you could arrange for the catheter bag to be removed as well?"

The nurse walks in, a small mirror clasped in her right hand. In one quick glance, she seems to take in the awkwardness of the situation, and the person causing it.

Dr. Jonas smiles over at the nurse. "Would you mind taking Mr. Thornton to the waiting area while we get Mrs. Thornton settled?"

The nurse nods. Extending her left arm, she guides him out of the room before he can voice his protests.

I point a finger at the closing door. "Why don't I remember him?"

The doctor looks at me, his features pinched. "What do you remember?"

"Nothing."

"Not to worry. It's probably transient global amnesia, due to the head injury you sustained. The amnesia is only a temporary episode. Symptoms last for around twenty-four hours. I'll order a CT."

The nurse walks back into the room and the doctor steps back as she draws the curtain and pulls back the bedlinen, exposing the catheter tube. Within seconds, the catheter is removed, and the curtain is whipped open.

The hand mirror sits on the bed, and my fingers trace the handle as Mr. Thornton walks back into the room. I get the distinct feeling he doesn't want to leave me alone with the doctor.

The pounding in my head gets worse. "Do you think I could have something for my headache?"

"Your medication will be here shortly. The nurses are just doing their rounds. Try to get some rest. Mr. Thornton." The doctor turns, nods at the stranger, and walks out of the room, nurse in tow.

I stare at the man as he takes a step closer to the bed. "I can't remember anything. I don't even know you."

His footsteps falter, and there is a sparkle in his eyes that wasn't there before. I get the impression my lack of memory makes him happy. It cements my earlier feelings that perhaps we are in the midst of a divorce and this momentary blip allows him to gain better control of the situation and me.

"Do you remember anything? The accident, me, our home?"

Despite the need to ask if he was listening to me, I shake my head. "The doctor says it's temporary, but he's ordering a CT scan to be on the safe side."

"You suffered a head injury, so what the doctor says makes sense."

The stranger appears more relaxed as he perches on the edge of my bed, taking my hand in his. His fingers are cool. What should be a comforting act agitates me.

The mirror is like a beacon. It's laughing at me for some reason. I try to relax and not pull my hand from Mr. Thornton's. I ignore the mirror's sniggers, waiting until I am alone to use it. Desperation is creeping in and I start wondering how quick I can get rid of him without appearing rude. Surely, he has a meeting to go to.

"I'm sorry, I don't know your name."

His smile doesn't reach his eyes. "My name is Liam."

"Right. I take it we're married."

The smile becomes tighter. "Yes."

"I'm sorry. This feels really strange."

"Don't worry. I am sure, like the doctor said, it's temporary, and you will soon be able to remember me and our life together."

His words and body language are at odds, and my anxiety deepens.

"Can you tell me how I ended up here?"

Liam looks uncertain, as though calculating the risk. I am convinced the risk he calculates has nothing to do with my health. Perhaps I am being unkind. I can't remember the person in front of me, I am only surmising.

He takes a breath, expelling it slowly. "I suppose it wouldn't hurt. You were mugged at the carpark on Piccadilly. According to the CCTV, as the man grabbed your bag, he pushed you down the concrete stairs, where you hit your head."

"Wow." Shock replaces my earlier unease. "I can see why I would want to forget."

"You were lucky, Kate. Your injuries could have been a lot worse."

Silence fills the small gap between us. "Is that my name? Kate?"

The name sounds familiar. My mind's reaction tells me I have a connection to it, though distant, not current. It could be that I am projecting this emotion.

Giving credence to the name would mean Liam is my husband, and I am not ready to accept him as such.

"Yes, that's your name." This time, his smile is genuine.

The door opens and a nurse walks in. There must have been a shift change as this one looks perky. Her hair is in a neat bun and her makeup is fresh.

"Hello. I've brought your medication."

I turn to Liam. "Do you mind if I rest for a while? I'm so tired."

He doesn't look impressed by my request, but he nods. "I will come again tonight. Jenny is desperate to see you. I will

14

bring her with me, unless you feel it will be too much."

"Who's Jenny?"

"Jenny is my sister, though she seems to be more *your* sister than mine. You're close."

I nod. "Right. This is crazy. My life is a blank canvas. I feel everyone knows more about me than I do."

"It's not forever, Kate. You will need to be patient."

"You're right. Let Jenny come with you. It might help clear some of the fog."

As Liam gets up to leave, he leans over and drops a light kiss on my forehead. I try not to shrink away from him. Without my memory, he is nothing more than a stranger. One, it would appear, I am still married to and not divorcing.

The door closes behind him and my shoulders lose some of their tension.

The nurse remains standing by the bed, waiting for me to take the medication. Reaching over, I take the proffered pills, swilling them down with some water.

She smiles and walks out the door.

And, once again, I am left alone with my thoughts.

The mirror has stopped laughing at me. A feeling of control replaces some of my uncertainty. *I* make the decision to look at my reflection, at the person sitting in this bed, no one else. Fear is a funny thing and, although I am desperate to look at myself, I wait. Part of me recognises that my memory may still be lost to me, and the person in the mirror might remain as much of a stranger as Liam Thornton. I may not even, on seeing myself, know who I am. A shiver runs down my spine, and I let my gaze fall on the window. The rain has stopped and a rainbow streams across the blue sky.

I allow the medication to take effect before picking up the mirror. My heart beats rapidly and my hands shake. It started out as a good idea, threaded with impatience, but now I want to procrastinate further. In the past ten minutes, I have scolded myself several times. *It's a stupid mirror! Get a grip, Kate!* (The name, though familiar, still doesn't seem to fit me.) *Come on, you can do this!*

I raise the mirror and look at the white plastic casing. All I have to do now is turn it round. It takes another five minutes before I get the nerve to do it. My eyes snap shut as the mirror spins, and I have to force my eyelids apart.

My mouth drops open and I look at the woman staring back at me. She is breathtakingly beautiful. Chastising myself for my vanity, I take a closer look at my face.

The caramel skin, oval face, high cheekbones, silky black hair, and slightly slanted almond eyes emphasise my Asian heritage. My eyes are green, demonstrating my mixed race, though it is clear from my other features that my Asian heritage is stronger.

Lifting the bedlinen, I take note of my small but muscular frame. I must exercise on a regular basis. Running, perhaps – running feels right.

After a prolonged moment of twisting my head this way and that and admiring myself in the mirror (I am conscious of being vain) I have made no progress in kickstarting my memory. My mind is as blank as when I woke. The notion is depressing.

Placing the mirror on the cupboard by the bed, I turn to the pink door. It provides no enlightenment, though my continued stare makes my eyes heavy. Pressing down on the button, the bed lowers. Sleep soon claims me, and my dreams are as blank and dark as my life appears to be.

Chapter Two

JESSICA

A re you sure this is going to work?" I look at Charles. His hazel eyes soften at my distress. Pushing his leather chair back from the old mahogany pedestal desk, he walks towards me. His ink-black hair falls to the collar of his white shirt, his golden tanned skin standing out against the fabric. He is built like a rugby player. Broad shoulders and thick muscle on a six-foot-six frame. But, more importantly, he makes me feel safe, something I haven't felt in such a long time. Charles is an oncology consultant at York Hospital.

The thought of what we're doing makes me nervous – more than our affair. But we have gone too far to stop now. Only a few days remain, and I will be free.

"He trusts me, Jess. He'll never suspect a thing." His hand brushes back my long black hair.

"I know, but still, it's the cancer part of our deception that torments me. I can't believe Liam bought it. But worst of all is lying about having cancer." The cracks are beginning to eat away at me, and the severity of this particular lie makes me extremely uncomfortable.

"It's the only way he will let you go."

I nod, recognising my desperation.

Liam is not the type of man you walk out on. People who betray or double-cross him have a tendency to die or disappear.

I am Liam's wife, and though I feel neither one of us ever loved the other, there was a time I thought I *could* love him if he had allowed me inside. For Liam, marrying me was about staking his claim. As his wife, I became his possession. Liam is a collector of rare and exquisite things. I see that now. Me, I was too confused at the time to understand what real love was about.

Liam is rich. I confused the gifts he gave me as love. When you have nothing, and are not used to having anything, it is easy to be overwhelmed when someone plies you with pretty items and attention. And that's what Liam did. I never stopped to think about what I was getting myself into. Liam, well, he got what he wanted – a beautiful and exotic wife to parade around his elite circle of friends.

I catch my reflection in the window as the early evening sky darkens. Soft almond-shaped emerald eyes stare back at me. My hair spills over my right shoulder and down my back. At five feet four inches, I am small, and my bone structure is delicate. My Asian heritage is easy to see, though my mixed cultural background is also evident. I hold a strong resemblance to mum, but my green eyes I get from my dad. Both my parents are dead. They died in a car crash when I was a little girl. Liam took advantage of my youth and innocence, as well as the pain of losing so much as a child. By the time I realised this, it was far too late.

Liam taught me how to dress and the etiquette required to move within the high-class circuit. By polishing away my rough edges, Liam ensured my acceptance in his inner circle, and I became the perfect Stepford wife. It didn't take me long to work out my mistake.

The pale-pink cropped Chanel trousers and white silk shirt I am wearing mean nothing to me – despite the price tag – other than serving as a reminder of the prisoner I have become under Liam's reign.

I am aware of the impeccable image we present as we circulate through charity events and walk with the elite. Men stare at Liam with unconcealed jealousy, and women are openly aggressive towards me. Liam soaks this up, like a man sucking energy directly from the national grid.

I knew when I met Charles Cavendish that there was an attraction. A spark between us. Charles is the closest friend Liam has. I knew better than to enter a relationship with him, to give in to my desires. But I did, and so did Charles, and I am not sorry. I feel no guilt over our affair. For the first time, I am loved, and it has nothing to do with the way I look and everything to do with the person I am.

My heart flutters as I look across at Charles. We never intended to fall in love. Charles isn't an easy man to resist. He is everything Liam isn't – quick to laugh, kind, and caring.

As he stops in front of me, I smile and trace a long delicate finger across his jawline.

His face lights up at my touch.

Sliding my arms over his broad shoulders, I wrap them around his neck. My feet nearly leave the floor as he hugs me to him. Breathing in his musky scent, I close my eyes and remind myself why I am doing this.

"It's going to be OK," Charles breathes into my neck.

I have no choice but to trust Liam will never find out what we are doing. He will kill us both if he does.

Liam has bought and manipulated his way through life. I am but a trinket to him, part of his expensive collection of fine art. And, like all of Liam's possessions, only *he* has the power to decide when one of them is no longer required. No one else plays with Liam's toys and lives.

My terminal cancer diagnosis relinquishes Liam's hold on me. Only death can free me – or, in my case, faking death. There are still a few things that Liam cannot control. Terminal cancer is one of them.

What Charles and I are doing is horrible but, as I said, we are desperate. I apologise daily to all those suffering from and who have died as a result of the disease. To the families whose lives have been ripped apart by cancer. But what is left for me to do? Do I accept that I have made my bed and now must lie in it, or do I take action and allow myself to live past my mistake and unhappiness?

Liam is my cancer, and I want rid of it. Selfishly, I want to live and be happy. To love as well as feel loved. While my morals battle with my actions, I find I want my freedom and happiness more than my principals.

I have been coming to Charles' clinic for a while now. The clinic not only adds to our cover story, but it is one of the few places we can meet without causing suspicion.

Charles is leaving York in two days to work at a clinic on the Isle of Skye, in Scotland. The clinic is new, and the opportunity will allow Charles and I to live together under my new identity.

Jake McCloud arranged for the papers allowing me to

change my name and open a bank account in the name Jessica Ripley. Charles now calls me Jess rather than Kate, to allow us to practice using my new name. Soon, 'Kate Thornton' will be no more.

Liam trusts no one, not even Charles, despite them being friends since senior school. Charles says Liam was different back then, back when they were boys. I don't know what changed. I only know the icy thread of greed and fortune has a firm hold of Liam now. There is no longer room for true friendship, or love.

The memory of telling Liam my cancer diagnosis stays with me.

He looks as if he will combust with outrage on the spot. Grabbing my arm, he marches me out of our luxurious – if barren – home, into his Bentley, straight to the clinic.

As Liam throws open the door to Charles' office, Charles' receptionist rushes forward, panicking. Liam neither takes the time to acknowledge her presence nor answer her cries of indignation, demanding that Charles cure me.

Charles walks around his desk to greet us, motioning for his receptionist to leave, and closes the door. He indicates that we should take a seat, but Liam remains standing, a firm grip on my arm, forcing me to stay on my feet, too.

"I'm sorry, Liam, there is no cure. Kate has a rare form of cancer known as Hodgkin lymphoma. This develops within the lymphatic system. There were a number of treatments available to Kate, and I did recommend chemotherapy when Kate was first diagnosed. However, she refused. The latest chest x-ray shows the cancer has now spread throughout her lymphatic system and is present in her organs.

"I'm sorry, there is nothing medical I can offer, other than

making her as comfortable as possible."

Liam's anger is like a storm threatening to unleash itself upon us. He lets go of my arm and paces the floor. Liam doesn't want a sick wife. Sympathy is not an emotion he cares to have directed his way.

I sink into a chair and rock back and forth, praying for forgiveness.

To survive Liam is to study him, to get to know and understand the monster who dwells within his impeccable appearance and the sharply cut, expensive two-piece Kiton suit. To a degree, I know how his devious mind works. The small insignificant signs that he tries to hide. It's good Liam has never taken the time to learn more about me. Otherwise, he might have noticed the small lines of worry creeping along my brow, or the nervous way my fingers twitch in my lap.

Charles has noticed. His hazel eyes tell me this will be over soon, and we will be free to start our life together. Seeing my inner torment, his fingers play with the pen in his hand, keeping them busy so they won't grab me and hug me to him.

"So, how long has she got?" Distain vibrates in Liam's voice as he nods his head in my direction, refusing to look at me.

"It's difficult to say, but I would estimate three months."

"Three months. Hmm, with such a short life span, there is no point prolonging the evitable with more treatment. The last thing I need is for her hair to be falling out."

Charles can't stop the way his jaw drops onto his chest at Liam's words.

Even as prepared as I am, I can't help feeling tossed aside as my usefulness disintegrates.

"Liam, Kate's your wife, *not some…"*

"And now she'll soon be dead," Liam bites out.

Charles' jaw snaps shut as Liam's attention swings in my direction.

"Find a clinic that will take her within the next few weeks. There's no point in her staying here. People will only talk, and I can do without that."

Looking at Charles, Liam runs a hand over the lapels of his suit. "Let me know the cost and I'll have the money wired over."

Shame engulfs me. It is one thing to know you are worthless, but to have it demonstrated so callously is hard to deal with, emotionally. Liam is unaware my cancer diagnosis isn't real, and I cannot prevent the shockwaves threading their way through my system.

The door slams behind Liam, and I bury my head in my hands and cry.

That day still affects me, even now. And though I know what Charles and I are doing is right, I can't embrace the fact that I have used cancer to gain my freedom.

However, I will not replace one prison for another. Thanks to Liam, there little time left before Kate Thornton makes her way to the clinic to 'die'. There is still a lot for me to sort out before Jessica Ripley can begin her new life.

Chapter Three

LIAM

Weeks after learning of Kate's cancer diagnosis, my outrage still simmers. Perhaps my anger is displaced, but I cannot believe what the bitch has done to me. My research confirms what Charles has told me about Hodgkin lymphoma. It doesn't lessen my anger, however.

I contemplate my misfortune as I sit in the courtyard at the Judge's Lodging, on Lendal, in the heart of York's city centre. The sun beats down on my navy two-piece ZILLI suit. Swirling my second gin and tonic round the glass, I am aware that there are only two days before Kate departs. I still have no solution to my current problem.

The other issue eating at me is my regret about making Kate my wife. Her low-class background is beneath me. My need to add her to my collection of exquisite objects overrode my judgement and distain of the lower-class. Giving in to my desire to own her, I have allowed her uniqueness to rule my head. Kate's beauty singles her out above women of every class and background.

When I orchestrated our first meeting, I already knew Kate's parents and adoptive parents were dead. Her aunt on her father's side had come forward, offering to care for her. How the social-care system deemed the aunt fit to care for Kate is a matter of debate, given the aunt's drug addiction.

As I rue my decision to marry Kate, I tap the brown file on the table in front of me. I often use the private detective services of Pete Townsend in my business transactions. It helps me remain a step ahead. Pete's report confirms the untimely death of both her birth and adoptive parents, and how Kate and her sister, Chrissie, were taken into their aunt's care. There is little information recorded in the file about Chrissie, other than that she went missing while she was living with her aunt. Social services and the police files provide no indication what happened to her. Her name, like so many, remains on the list of missing persons.

My desire to own Kate did not stop me from employing Pete's services. I hate surprises. Kate is no different than any business transaction. If you make just one exception, you open yourself up to failure. The money at my disposal is a tribute to the unemotional way I choose to live. Emotional attachments are foolish and costly, and I am above such things.

Death follows Kate. It is an oversight, on my part, that I did not recognise this. It is unusual for a child to lose two sets of parents. I chastise myself for not considering this at the time.

The ice is melting and the water content in the glass increases, diluting the gin further.

It is not Kate's cancer that bothers me, so much as the fact that it is taking her from me and therefore stripping away my control over her. I should have chosen to remain single, eliminating this kind of situation.

Changing the past isn't an option, so the question remains, what am I going to do about Kate?

Raising the glass to my lips, I empty its contents. It is time for me to take action. At present, I am unsure what that action will be. Still, I cannot sit here all day.

As I reach for the file, I notice Kate walking down the street. Her long black hair swishes down her back, cascading from a high ponytail. My right eyebrow raises. The clothes are high-street trash, not the expensive designer names I like Kate to wear. I watch her turn, hooking her arm through that of the man walking at her side.

Kate looks happier than I have ever seen her. My anger spikes as I watch them. The bitch is having an affair! A snigger falls from my lips. Despite the cancer, I add her death to my to-do list. No, not only *her* death. Also the man she is having the affair with. And I will ensure that Kate understands she is responsible.

Removing my mobile from the inside pocket of my jacket, I place the file back on the table. I wait for them to come closer so I can get a clear photograph. I don't recognise the man, but I know a detective who will provide all the information I need to give my hitman, Jeff Green.

The phone rings. I send it an irritated glance. I'm about to ignore the call when I see Kate's name on the screen. My eyes cut back to the woman lazily walking down Lendal, and who is now kissing the man.

Accepting the call, Kate's voice filters through.

"Liam?" The woman in front of me continues kissing the man, confirming she isn't Kate.

I had to be sure. See the evidence before I make my next move.

"Not now." Kate is sputtering as I terminate the call. I take a picture as my brain processes what this means.

The woman passes, and I sit down. A waitress scurries over to the table next to mine, and I stop her mid stride, ordering another gin and tonic.

Opening the file, I look at Pete's report. While a sister is mentioned, there are no photographs, nor is there an age or date of birth. At the time, this missing information didn't bother me. Now, it sends anger slithering through my veins. The answer to the problem of Kate's coming death should have been contained in this file, not left to a chance encounter. The oversight is going to cost Pete, but for now, I smile. The sister isn't just Kate's younger or elder sibling. No, she is her twin. Her *identical* twin.

I flip through the photos I have taken, cropping and enlarging the woman's face on the screen. There is no telling them apart. For the first time since getting Kate's cancer diagnosis, my body relaxes.

The waitress sets my gin and tonic on the table and I dial Pete's number.

"I've sent you a number of photos. You need to start explaining why you failed to tell me that Kate has an identical twin sister."

Pete owes me, and I am collecting my debt – plus interest.

No one feeds me incorrect information without paying the price, and Pete is about to discover that price. With Charles leaving to go live in some godforsaken remote place in Scotland, there is no one to stop me.

The phone echoes with the urgent fumbling of a man not prepared to accept his fate. My lips grow thinner.

"Well, I haven't got all day. Frankly, I've waited long enough. How many years is it since you compiled the information on Kate for me?" I don't wait for Pete to answer. "I'll tell you, Pete. Six years. *Six years*, and in that time, you never bothered to check that the information I paid for was complete. You know I'm not a tolerant man, Pete. Tolerance is for fools, and I will not be treated like a fool."

"You didn't specify how far back to go, so I only did a preliminary scan of the time before Kate was taken in by her aunt. I *did* inform you about the sister. The aunt sold her to a couple who couldn't have children. You weren't interested in the sister at the time."

I put down my glass with a thud. The occupants of a table near me look over but are soon engrossed in their conversation once again.

"Don't you *ever* try and weasel your way into thinking that this is my fault. It's not going to go away that easily. The issue here isn't whether I was interested in the sister at the time or not, it's that you should have done your job properly. You didn't, you were sloppy, and now you owe me."

"Mr. Thornton…" Pete stutters, and I can sense him gathering his excuses.

"I wouldn't go down that road if I were you, Pete. People like you are ten a penny. You have no living relatives, no wife or children. It's fair to say no one will miss you."

"Are you threatening me?" Pete sounds stunned.

The poor man really is stupid, despite being an excellent private detective. If he thinks his sloppy work won't have any consequences attached to it, he's a silly, silly, silly man.

"No, Pete, I'm not threatening you. I am *telling* you that you have twenty-four hours to finish getting all the information on Kate and her sister. And, to clarify – when I say *all* the information, I mean down to blood type and pimples, or you can kiss your existence goodbye. I hope I have made myself understood."

"Yes." Pete bites out the word like someone is holding a gun to his head and threatening to pull the trigger.

The image makes me smile.

"Good. I shall see you tomorrow at ten a.m. sharp, at my office."

"But that's only sixteen hours away." At least Pete can do the maths.

"Then you'd better get going, before I move our meeting forward." I hang up, leaving Pete spluttering into his phone.

Picking up my drink, I start working out my options.

First things first. I have to get the real Kate out of the way and into her final resting place. I will have to curb my impatience and ride out the forty-eight hours left.

The sun no longer feels unwelcome. Like my brightening mood, I find its radiance has a warming effect.

Chapter Four

JESSICA

I don't know, Charles, something's wrong."
From where I'm sitting on the bed, I have a clear view across the lawn through the patio doors. The gardens are breath-taking. The flowerbeds are in full bloom, producing a kaleidoscope of colour and beckoning scents. Fourteen acres of land spread out before me. Two acres are manicured, well-cultivated lawns and flowerbeds, the rest is split into pastures and woodland. A stream and a small humpbacked bridge signal the end of the property.

Jake McCloud, the gardener – and provider of my false identity – is busy plucking weeds and deadheading flowers. Though arthritis causes his hands to curl in on themselves, Jake is the happiest person I have ever met.

Jake has worked for Liam since forever. Despite his sharp mind, Jake's age and health make him slow at his job, and his continued employment contradicts Liam's shrewd and calculating mind. I find this behaviour of Liam's odd and difficult to understand or accept.

Jake Junior (as he is referred) is a recent addition to Liam's small household. His employment arises from Jake's need for assistance. This I find fascinating, though my probing has never revealed the reason for Liam's uncharacteristic behaviour.

I open the patio door, lean over the balcony, and watch the men work. I will miss this pair. Tears fill my eyes. Twenty-four hours to go and all this will end. The house, with its expensive furnishings and fine artwork, mean nothing to me, but Jake and I are friends.

Over the last six years, Jake has been my confidante. I have confessed my affair with Charles to him, and our plan to escape Liam. And my longing to find my sister, Chrissie. His snow-topped head has bobbed with understanding, and his tanned arms have held me tight while I cried.

I am not saying goodbye to a dear friend, but to family. And, having no close blood relatives, the pain of leaving Jake behind, knowing I will never contact or see him again, rips at my heart.

Leaving the doors open, I flop back down on the bed. "Liam has asked me to leave my rings."

"You're worrying too much, Jess. You were never going to take your rings."

"I know, but doesn't it seem odd to you? It's not as though they hold any sentimental value to Liam, and he doesn't need the money. Why now, Charles? Why not tell me to leave them when I told him which hospice I was going to? Why now? It doesn't make any sense." I try to breathe through my rising anxiety.

A wealth of princess diamonds runs around the entire platinum wedding band. A six-carat princess-diamond engagement ring catches the sun, and the wall in front of me dances with colour.

"Slow down, Jess. You're probably reading too much into it." Charles' deep tones sound in my ear.

"You could be right." I try to relax, but it isn't happening.

"Has anything else happened?"

"No, though he's been looking at me oddly lately. He just sort of *stares*, and then smiles. I don't think he was even listening when I told him about the hospice. So why the rings? Why now? I feel like he knows something and is biding his time, waiting to pounce."

Charles chuckles down the phone. "You make him sound like a panther."

"More like a hyena."

"Come on, everything is going to be fine. This time tomorrow, you will arrive at the hospice, and then on to your new life. Just twenty-four hours, Jess, that's all we have to wait."

I smile into the phone. "I know. I guess I'm just feeling jittery."

"It's to be expected."

"Charles, thanks for listening."

I sense him smile. It causes a bubble of warmth and joy to burst inside me.

"Hey, there's no need for that, it's what I'm here for."

My heart flips in my chest as happiness explodes. "I love you," I whisper.

"I love you too, Jess. Now, if I'm not mistaken, the lady has a lot of packing to do."

I laugh. "True."

"Right. Come then. Until tomorrow."

"Until tomorrow, Charles."

I place the phone on the hook and look round my room. Heading over to the walk-in wardrobe, I pull back the double doors and step inside. The room is filled with designer labels. Armani, Stella McCartney, Gucci, and Chanel hang on the racks. Beneath them are matching shoes and handbags. Plonking myself onto the long bench in the centre of the room, I look at the clothes. I won't be taking any of them with me. Instead, I reach above them to the shelf where I have buried a number of outfits.

Inside the plastic bags is comfortable high-street clothing. Jessica Ripley has a taste for comfort – flowing cotton dresses, black leggings, jeans. And flat shoes. She is a down-to-earth girl who prefers the ordinary above the elite.

Folding my new clothes into the waiting suitcase, my fear still eating at my nerves. I watch my hands shake. It is the thought of discovery, and nothing more than that, I try to tell myself. Charles is right, of course. There is nothing to worry about. In twenty-four hours, I will be free.

Once I've finished packing, I make my way downstairs, conscious of my need for space. The house is becoming oppressive, and I need to get away, to sit and breathe in the fresh country air and collect my thoughts. My footsteps echo on the marble flooring. The staircase sweeps up from both sides of the hall, announcing its presence with grandeur and elegance. A large crystal chandelier hangs from the ceiling, off which smaller crystals tumble down in tiny droplets.

Everything Liam does, he does with style, hiring the best there is to ensure his expectations are met. This house is no exception, perfectly tailored to Liam's wants and desires. The building is imposing with its white-painted exterior and crisp, stylish interior. Antiques litter the house – a statement of power.

The house boasts fourteen bedrooms across two wings, all ensuite. The large ostentatious kitchen houses top-of-the-line gadgets that would be the envy of any chef. The house was constructed to be lavish. It wasn't built with a heart. It lacks the thing that makes a house a *home* – a soul.

The building is as polished and cold as Liam.

Fine art hang from the walls. Rembrandts, Van Goghs. Not a single personal photograph litters any of the antique sideboards or tables. It is all rather sad. Photographs are memories. Times to remember with fondness.

The missing photographs say a lot about Liam, and our relationship.

I walk through the front door, car keys in my right hand. Outside, a silver Aston Martin glistens in the sun. It is a lovely car, but to me, it represents yet another item Liam has collected.

I smile to myself. At least this collector's item is getting out.

Sliding into the leather seat, I fire up the engine. It roars to life. The tyres eat up the miles like a kid eats its way through a box of chocolates.

Liam might think he owns me, but I have learnt a thing or two from him.

He is content to throw money at all his investments, so long as they perform. And, so long as I looked elegant and sophisticated, he was happy for me to spend large amounts of cash. Taking advantage of this, I have been building myself a nest egg so I can support myself in my new life.

Jessica Ripley is a woman of means.

A smile spreads across my lips at the thought.

A white farmhouse sits on the Isle of Skye, open to the elements. The grassland surrounding it leads down to the beach.

Proportionally, the rooms are small, but the important thing is that the farmhouse has a soul.

This farmhouse is the home of Jessica Ripley and Charles Cavendish. And, together, they are going to fill it with laughter and love.

My fears over Liam melt away as I turn on the radio. Def Leppard's 'Let's Get Rocked' fills the car, and I start singing along.

As the saying goes, 'When one door closes, another one opens.'

Chapter Five

LIAM

At 10 a.m., the door to my office opens and Peter Townsend walks in. I remain seated and wait for him to approach. A brown file is placed on my desk, and I gesture with my right hand for Pete to take a seat.

My fingers tap the file as Pete makes himself comfortable in one of the black leather chairs in front of the desk. The seven-foot antique Victorian oak desk separates us by over four feet.

I have a passion for collecting the best, and my office space is no exception. The large window on my left looks out on the River Ouse. It flows through the centre of York, on which tour boats brimming with happy tourists chug along. The midmorning sun lights up the office, bouncing off the Farrow & Ball ash-grey painted walls. At the rear of the thirty-foot room, two Berwick Chesterfield ox-blood sofas face each other. On one wall, shadows caress a Rembrandt. Four Victorian filing cabinets with brass handles cover the wall to the right of my desk.

I don't believe in littering my desk with personal photographs, so the only items on the deep-red leather top are my Apple laptop and an eighteen-carat rose-gold Caran d'Ache Caelograph Zenith fountain pen. I pick the pen up and roll it between my fingers. The twenty-two diamonds on its body sparkle in the sunlight.

I am aware that the sparseness of my office makes people uncomfortable. Clutter can tell you a lot about a person and is the reason I can't abide it.

Pete is sweating as I open the file and begin reading the contents. My continued silence eats away at his nerves.

"Her name is Chrissie Sanders."

I look up from the file and Pete plays with the collar of his shirt.

At six foot six and weighing in at over two hundred pounds, Pete looks intimidating. A scar runs across his left cheek, and his crooked nose adds to the hardness. His deep-set brown-black eyes stare at me with uncertainty. He keeps his hair military short, in keeping with his threatening image.

Pete looks uncomfortable. Gone is his usual confident swagger. He has replaced his normal loose-fitting clothes with a drab black polyester suit that is far too small for his broad, thick-set shoulders. The cheap fabric of his jacket stretches over the girth of his arms, and his trousers pull at the thighs.

Pete loosens the skinny grey tie, highlighting his nervousness.

I look down at the file, allowing the silence to infiltrate further.

Pete's dancing legs beat against the oak floor.

The exertion of power over another is about emphasizing their weaknesses without verbalising that you're doing so. Power is a delicate form of manipulation. It takes strength and self-control, and above all, it is about never relinquishing the control you have – *any* of it.

Pete's tanned skin loses colour as I raise my eyes and close the file. My left hand lingers on it as I take the Caran d'Ache and begin writing a few notes. I acknowledge to myself that Pete has surpassed himself. Not only has he provided the information I asked for, including blood type, he has provided Chrissie's home address, mobile and landline numbers, her place of work, routine, and timelines. Fear is a very motivational emotion.

"You have outdone yourself, Pete." I allow my compliment to ease some of Pete's nerves.

Placing the pen on the surface of my desk, I lean back in my chair, my fingers touching as I tap them against my lips. "Now, there is the matter of your debt."

Pete sputters, "W-What debt? I've provided the information you asked for, at no cost."

The smile dancing beneath my skin never reaches my lips. Instead, shake my head. "Six years too late, Pete."

Silence settles as a mixture of emotions cloud Pete's face. Sweat trickles from his temples, down past his ears.

When I speak, I ensure my voice is even and carries a reasonable tone. "If I add up the interest on the payment I made, well, you can understand when I say I'm out of pocket. You took my money, Pete, and didn't do the job you were paid to do. That's an awful lot of interest, especially at my rates. And now you're going to pay some of it back."

"What do you want?"

I like a man who knows when he's beaten.

I open the file, never allowing any of the pleasure I feel to show. Sorting through the paperwork, I select a photograph. "I want *her*." Placing the photograph of Chrissie's smiling face on the desk, I tap the paper. "And you're going to ensure I get her."

Pete pales. Sweat pours down his face like tears.

I make a mental note to tell my receptionist-cum-secretary to get the cleaners to disinfect the chair.

"I don't understand, Mr. Thornton. I can't just kidnap her."

My forehead wrinkles in confusion. I disagree with Pete's statement. If I instructed him to kidnap Chrissie, that is exactly what he would do.

"Who said anything about kidnapping? Your problem, Pete, is you have no diplomacy. You're like a bulldozer."

Pete's brow wrinkles.

"You, Pete, are going to push her down the stairs at that multi-storey car park in the Coppergate Centre where she leaves her car every Wednesday, making sure she hits her head hard"

"I'm sorry, I don't understand," Pete interrupts me.

"Then I suggest you stop talking and let me finish," I snap.

Pete shrinks into the leather chair.

"Amnesia, Pete. That is what I am talking about."

"A-A-Amnesia? But what happens if it doesn't work?"

"The way I see it, Pete, you have a fifty-fifty chance of it working. Let's just hope, for your sake, that the coin lands in your favour. If it doesn't, you won't need to worry about next month's rent. Therefore, I would ensure you make the encounter as traumatic as possible. According to my medical research trauma is linked to amnesia."

Since seeing Chrissie, I have done a lot of research into amnesia. Unlike Pete, I have taken all the possibilities into account. The greater the trauma, the greater the likelihood of the brain closing off certain memories. Add a good whack to the head and the odds are stacked even more in my favour.

The brain is cunning in the way it shuts out traumatic events. Anne Clark, my PA, was the one to give me the idea of amnesia. She was recently involved in a car accident. Her broken body lies in a hospital bed, but she doesn't recall the crash. It is also the reason I have a receptionist / secretary at present, rather than a PA.

Should Chrissie retain any memories, I can explain them away. I have worked it all out. There's a niggling feeling at the back of my head, telling me I am a desperate man.

It is going to work. It *has* to work. Medical professionals may argue with my plan, but there is no room for failure, and a positive attitude must be maintained.

With Kate dying, and upon seeing Chrissie, one thing is clear – I am not prepared to lose twice.

"How can I make her memories disappear? Amnesia isn't a precise condition. There are no guarantees."

"That is not my problem."

"B-But you're being unreasonable."

"If I were unreasonable, Pete, you would be lying in the morgue right now."

Pete's jaw snaps shut and the light in his eyes dies. "I wish I'd never met you."

If I sniffed the air, I would find the scent of a condemned man.

"Well, you did."

The big man in front of me looks much smaller than he

did when he walked in here.

"Like it or not, Pete, I own you." Picking up the photograph from the desk, I place it back in the file.

Pete's shoulders slump and his eyes never leave the floor.

"Don't let me down, Pete, not this time."

He nods.

"You had better go. You have a lot of organising to do before Wednesday."

The door closes behind Pete's retreating form.

I open my laptop and study my calendar. There is only one event that requires my attendance and Kate's. It is Janine Walters' charity ball over at Merchant Adventures. The woman is middle-class trash trying to become something she can never be – high-class. She'll accept my apologies when she hears of Kate's accident.

Chapter Six

KATE

f there are any changes or you start remembering anything, please contact us."

I nod to the policemen as they close the door behind them.

The sun floods into the hospital room, and I want to scream at it. Having spent the past hour saying, *Sorry, I can't remember,* to the policemen's questions, my frustration is reaching the boiling point.

My handbag was found, though its contents remain missing. I am not expecting to ever see them again, nor do I feel anything over their loss. They wouldn't mean anything to me, anyway, given that I am suffering from amnesia.

Liam has thoughtfully brought in our wedding album to see if it will assist with my recall. It now sits on the end of the bed. If books could laugh, the white leather-bound album would be howling, tears pouring from it. Of course, Liam's thoughtfulness serves a dual purpose. Not only does it make him look considerate, it also confirms I am Mrs. Thornton.

It is strange that the person in the wedding album remains such a mystery to me, given that it is *my* wedding. The stunning vintage lace Eliza Jane Howell wedding dress I am wearing, with its delicate pearl and crystal beading, increases my frustration. It does not kindle any memory or attraction I might have felt for Liam. Instead, it painfully reminds me that I am nothing more than an outsider at my own wedding, and life.

"Kate..." The gentle hand Jenny lays on my arm indicates she has been calling my name for some time.

I muster a smile, placing my hand on top of hers. "Sorry, Jenny, I was lost in thought."

"It's going to be OK. You know that, don't you?"

The impulse to tell her nothing is OK rises. I swallow it down, aware none of this is Jenny's fault.

"I know I'm being silly, letting it all upset me." This time when I smile it is genuine. "So, come on, tell me how the arrangements are going. Is the nursery finished?"

Jenny sits back in her chair, her hand resting on her swelling stomach. "I'm nearly there. Well, I probably *am* there, but I always think of something else to buy."

When Jenny walked into my room, I hadn't been prepared for the stab of pain her pregnant form would ignite within my heart. My emotional torment at seeing Jenny still puzzles me. I know from Liam that we have been married six years and we don't have, or intend to have, children. Yet the feelings battling for release inside me keep telling me something is wrong. Did I want children? The possibility is high. It is natural that, at some point, a woman will want a child. So, is it Liam who doesn't want children? He doesn't strike me as the dad type. I think this is the most likely scenario, rather than me not wanting children or not being capable of having them.

However, my head – being the torturer that it is – keeps telling me this feeling isn't about having children, but that I *have* a child. If I close my eyes, there is a shadow there. The whispering voice of a child that keeps crying out for her mummy. I rub my head. I am so confused, and nothing is making sense.

Doubt and confusion wriggle inside me constantly. The worst is the part of myself that keeps telling me – despite the evidence sitting on the end of the bed, I am not Kate – that this is not my life. But if this life isn't mine, whose is it? It isn't as if Liam has stalked the hospital wards waiting for some poor unfortunate soul to lose their memory and has swooped in and claimed her. Jenny isn't part of some conspiracy. The wedding album, Jenny, and Liam tell me I am Kate Thornton. Perhaps I should ask my brain very nicely to switch off and accept that this is my life. I am married to Liam, whom it is obvious I don't love, or even like.

Jenny yawns and her bright-blue eyes shimmer. "Oh, dear, sorry. It's past my nap time."

"Why don't you go? You can't be comfy sat in that chair."

Jenny shakes her head, sending her light-brown hair swinging about her jaw. "As alluring as my bed is, I'd best stay. Liam asked me to wait with you while he called at the house to get you some fresh clothes."

I try to keep my face neutral.

"Look, Jenny, it's not like I'm going to leave here before he comes back. As nice as these silk Rosamosario pyjamas are," I lift the nude-coloured fabric away from my chest, "people are going to notice."

"It's OK. Besides, you're going home today. That has got to be huge for you, given that you can't remember anything. I want to be here to support you."

'Home' is a funny word when you have no memory. It's supposed to be a place of enjoyment and happiness. It is a place where you are loved, respected, and cared for. A family space. None of these feelings apply, in my case. How can they... if I can't remember it?

The thought of being home alone with Liam makes me nervous, and a thread of fear flickers through me, making my stomach flip unhappily. Given my lack of attraction towards him, I'm certainly not going to have sex with him. Not that Liam has made advances, or even hinted at it. Still, it is what married couples do. He must have expectations.

Aghhh!!!! How I hate the conflict that eats at me.

My head flops back against the pillows. "Other than missing your nap, how are you doing? You can't have long to go now." I point to her belly.

"Scared."

"It's the second time round you need to worry about. Now *that's* scary because you know what to expect." I am not going to ask myself why I said that, or even why I know.

"There isn't going to be a second time. I think this is going to be it."

"You don't mean that. What happened to the girl who said, ten minutes ago, that she wants at least six?"

Jenny giggles. "I've changed my mind."

"You can't do that. Ten minutes is too soon for changing your mind. You have to leave it at least a year or so, or until you start feeling broody again."

"Yeah, well, that's a pregnant lady for you. I'm forever changing my mind."

I look up at the ceiling. "You know, it's strange. I can tell you how it feels to be pregnant. How uncomfortable you feel the further along in the pregnancy you get. How it feels to want to sleep on your side but not being unable to because of your bump. I can tell you about the immense love you are going to feel for the little person inside you. And yet, I've never had kids, so why do I have these feelings?" Tears fall from the corners of my eyes.

Jenny reaches across, taking my hand. "I wish I had some answers for you, Kate, I really do."

I can hear the sadness in her voice and I feel mean and selfish for being the one to put it there.

"Don't worry, I'm just being silly. I'm going to be an aunt, which means I get to spoil my niece or nephew and fill them with sugar and hand them back to mum and dad."

"Don't you dare. And no drum kit, either."

"It's as well I'm not thinking of buying one, then. A drum kit is far too common a musical instrument for their Uncle Liam. No, I'm thinking of a violin, and the sweet sound of screeching strings," I tease Jenny.

She groans. "I think I'd rather have a drum kit."

"Well, I'm betting Uncle Liam won't."

The door opens and Liam appears. Our teasing chatter dies as he steps into the room.

A frown creases his otherwise-perfect skin. In his left hand is a Louis Vuitton Bowling Vanity bag. The monogrammed canvas is instantly recognisable. Liam has ditched his Armani suit for a navy dogtooth-patterned wool-and-silk-blend Tom Ford. I wonder if he owns a pair of jeans, or if he thinks they're too common. I'm sure Harrods sells jeans, so it isn't as if he'd have to walk the High Street.

"The doctor has signed you out. You can leave whenever

you're ready." He places the vanity bag on the bed, his sharp blue eyes looking from me to Jenny. His lips are thin, and a look of displeasure falls over his face.

Unzipping the bag, I look inside. I had no choice in the items Liam packed, and I wonder what designer wear he considers right for a wife with no memory and a bruised body. Pulling out a pair of cream linen wide-leg Chanel trousers and a pale-pink silk shirt with three-quarter sleeves, I eye them with suspicion. Even designers must make comfortable clothing to slob around in.

"Are we going out somewhere?"

Liam blinks at my question. "No."

Staring at the outfit, my fingers playing with the fabric of the silk blouse, I try to reconcile going home to rest with what is spread over the bed. I fail.

"Do I normally get this dressed up to sit around the house doing nothing?"

Jenny places a hand on my arm.

I ignore it.

Picking up the black-and-beige lambskin-and-grosgrain Chanel mules, I look at Liam. "Three-inch heels, Liam, really?"

"They are three-point-*three*-inch heels."

I stare at him with hostility. "Sorry, my mistake for missing the point three. Though it doesn't change the fact that they are impractical."

Liam's expression doesn't change, but the air in the room radiates with annoyance.

"Put the outfit on, Kate."

It appears my clothing is not up for discussion.

The mules drop from my fingertips, clattering to the floor. My green eyes lock on to his. "No."

"Unless you want to leave here in your pyjamas, I would put the outfit on."

Folding my hands over my chest, I toss my hair over my shoulder. "That's fine with me."

"Kate." My name sounds like a warning.

Jenny's hand returns to my arm. "Come on, Kate, the linen trousers will keep you cool. It's frightfully warm out there."

A loud sigh escapes my lips, and I grab the vanity bag along with the clothes. I leave the mules where I dropped them.

"Fine," I grind out. "But just so you know, I'm only doing this for you, Jenny."

Liam picks up the shoes and hands them to me. "Don't forget these."

I am tempted to shove the shoes up his backside, but I refrain. I walk past, leaving them dangling from his fingers.

Jenny takes them from Liam as she waddles to the bathroom. The door closes behind us.

"What just happened out there?" I ask Jenny as she lowers herself onto the pink plastic chair near the shower.

"I'm not sure. Maybe it's your head injury? You've never complained about getting dressed up before."

My jaw hangs open. "I am beginning to not like myself."

Jenny laughs. "I don't always like myself, either, but most of the time I make an effort to get along with myself."

"Hmph."

"Come on, you never know. You might feel better once you've changed." Jenny shrugs. "More *you*."

"The only thing that's going to make me feel better right now is punching Liam and wiping that smug look off his face."

Tears run down Jenny's face. "You are funny, Kate. I think I like this side of you."

"Hmph." I grab the outfit and strip out of my pyjamas, handing them to Jenny.

The woman in the mirror, like everything else, is a mystery to me. I am not even sure I want to know to her.

"Your makeup's here." Jenny hands me a small matching Louis Vuitton makeup bag.

"Thanks, Jenny, but I think I'll leave the makeup. Despite what Liam may think, I am going home to laze around."

Worry falls over Jenny's features. "I don't think I've *ever* seen you without makeup. Well, you know, apart from in here."

"Is that my choice, or his?"

"Kate, please. Liam is already upset."

"And what about me? He's not the one leaving the hospital draped in Chanel and forced to put his feet into three-point-*three*-inch-heel mules. Because we wouldn't want to miss the point three, would we?"

"Please."

"Oh, for goodness' sake. Fine. I'll put some makeup on. But I'm not getting completely made-up to sit in a garden chair and read a book or dream about wearing joggers."

A loud sigh escapes my lips and I turn to look at Jenny.

"I'm being grumpy and taking it out on you. I'm sorry."

Jenny smiles. "Don't worry. With everything that's going on right now, I'd say you are allowed to be grumpy."

I sit on the toilet lid, next to Jenny's chair. "What's with Liam? I don't get it. Whatever would possess him to think I would want to stick my feet into those mules or get dressed up? People don't stay in the hospital for a holiday, it's because they're sick."

"Liam has always been into appearances. I think he's afraid someone will take advantage of him, like they did with Dad. Life's easier if he keeps the world at arm's length."

"I don't think I want to feel sorry for him."

"You don't have to feel sorry for Liam. I don't think he even notices what he's doing." Jenny lets out a breath. "He's needed to control the world around him for so long, it's hard for him to let go. You have always accepted Liam's need for control in the past. I don't think I have ever seen you disagree with him before. You've always steered clear of conflict."

"You mean I'm a pushover."

"Not a pushover. Perhaps *compliant.*"

"I still sound like a pushover."

Jenny smiles. "Come on, things aren't so bad, and you do look gorgeous."

"Thanks, I think."

Grabbing the bag, I hold out my hand to Jenny. "Come on, let's get this over with. You're a nap down."

Liam is standing at the window, his hands clasped behind his back. He turns as I walk out with Jenny.

"You look lovely, Kate."

The three-point-three-inch-heels click against the tile flooring. Ignoring him, I turn and give Jenny a hug.

"Go on, home you and get some rest."

"OK, OK, I'm off." Jenny turns as she opens the door. "I'll call round and see you tomorrow."

I nod as I watch her waddle out the room, leaving me alone with Liam. My hands begin to sweat as I try not to think about the journey ahead of me.

Liam steps over and takes my left hand in his. Without a word, he places a diamond wedding band and a large diamond engagement ring on my finger. I feel like I have been branded.

Taking the vanity bag from my right hand, Liam places a hand beneath my elbow and steers me out of the room.

My shoes tap along the corridor. Fear craws along my skin with each step I take. No one stops us, though I want to scream for someone to help me, that this man is nothing more than a stranger. My back remains straight, and I refuse to give in to fear. Instead, I remind myself that Liam isn't a mass murderer. There is no way he would get his well-manicured hands dirty.

Liam's black Bentley is parked outside, and the boot flips open as we near. My heart thumps erratically, but somehow, I manage to sink into the leather seat without my legs shaking or crumbling out from under me.

As Liam starts the engine, I fix my eyes on the changing scenery.

* * *

An hour later, the car draws to a stop outside a monstrous large white building. The house spreads before me like an ivory palace. There is no spark of recognition. It is as if I am seeing it for the first time.

The car door opens and Liam helps me out. My feet move forward across the block paving to the large black front door. A voice in my head keeps telling me none of this is real, and I'll wake up soon. It never happens.

Liam swings the door open and together we step inside.

The interior is more sterile than the hospital I have just left. There are no personal photographs on display, and I am betting the paintings on the wall carry high price tags. The white marble beneath my feet adds to the coldness of the house, and the elaborate sweeping staircase looks as inviting as a pool full of alligators.

I stop in the large reception hall, my eyes lingering on a chandelier that pours down from the high ceiling in small droplets.

"Why are there no photographs?"

Liam guides me to the staircase. "We have paintings."

"Yes, I can see that, but it's very impersonal."

He continues pulling me up the stairs, and though I really don't want to go, I have no choice in the matter.

"Your bedroom is this way."

My feet come to an abrupt stop. "Pardon?"

Liam pulls me forward. "You can freshen up."

"I've only just gotten dressed."

Ignoring me, we come to a stop in front of a white door. My heart is pounding, and I think I am going to have a heart attack. I really don't want to be here. And definitely not with Liam.

The door opens and the bedroom looms in front of me.

"This is your room. Mine is in the north wing."

Surprise hits me and, before my brain engages, my mouth opens. "Why do we have separate rooms? Is there something wrong with us?"

"There is nothing wrong with our relationship, Kate. It is what it is."

"Right."

Liam's hand drops from my arm. He walks into the room placing the vanity bag on the bed. "I'll leave you to freshen up." He looks at his Rolex. "I have a meeting I need to prepare for. If you need anything, I will be in my study."

It does not occur to Liam that I don't know where his study is, and the door closes behind him.

Relief floods my body. Kicking off the mules, I walk over to the patio doors and look out across the garden. I give my brain a chance to take in the immaculate lawns and beautiful flowerbeds. There is no recognition.

Leaving the doors open, I turn and walk back into the bedroom. The room is large, and the bedroom furniture is proportional. Perfume and makeup clutter the dressing table, and there is a book on the bedside table. A bookmark indicates that I am halfway through it. I don't recall the author or title and resign myself to start at the beginning.

Two sets of double doors sit along the wall opposite the patio and balcony. Opening the first set, I peer into a bathroom. There is a large roll-top bath, walk-in shower, double sink and vanity, and toilet. The second set of doors opens into a walk-in wardrobe. Racks of designer clothes line up beside each other. Beneath them are shoes and handbags. A long, padded bench runs down the middle of the room.

My fingers touch the clothing. Not a single memory exists.

Deciding that I am going to need time to work out what to 'freshen up' into, I sit on the bench and stare at the array of clothes before me.

There are no joggers, other than running clothes, and while the thought of pulling on a pair of leggings appeals, I am conscious of the spike in Liam's blood pressure it would cause.

There is a time and place for battles. Today is not the day for creating unnecessary tension.

It takes me twenty minutes of staring and rummaging through the clothes to find something that I feel will make me more comfortable without antagonising Liam.

As I walk out of the bathroom, my hair still damp from

the shower, my face devoid of makeup, I slip on a paisley Etro maxi dress with kimono sleeves I have chosen as my 'freshen up' item. The dress has a bohemian feel to it and falls to the floor in electric-blue waves. The pure-silk lining caresses my bare legs.

While Liam's need for me to wear makeup lingers in the back of my mind, I choose to ignore it. Closing the bedroom door, I make my way downstairs. Book in hand, I begin my search for a garden chair to relax in.

A pair of Tom Ford sunglasses sit on top of my head. My bare feet make no sound on the marble floor as I try to find my way into the garden.

My brain niggles at me, but I refuse to listen. Life without a memory is frustrating, but I am not prepared to allow it to rip at my nerves until it becomes my one-and-only obsession. It will lead to a mental breakdown. Instead, I am going to live each day using my instincts. If something *feels* right, I shall accept that it is.

The knowledge that Liam will be sleeping in a different wing than me helps instil calm.

I make a number of wrong turns before I find my way outside. Closed doors all look the same. The rooms, though their functions are different, all have the same sterile atmosphere.

The sound of birds singing and the fresh scent of flowers and cut grass fill my senses as I walk across the patio area and settle myself into the beige rattan double-pod hanging chair.

Sliding the sunglasses over my eyes, I open the book. My hair tumbles about my waist, drying in the sun.

Chapter Seven

JESSICA

The smell of fresh-brewed coffee interrupts my sleep. I raise my hands above my head and stretch. A soft smile plays on my lips at the sound of footsteps on the landing and the clinking of cups. For a dead person, my health has never been better, and I am in an extremely good mood, feeling content and happy.

The sun shines through the open curtains on my right. If I opened the window birds would sing. My bare skin basks in the warmth and my inner self radiates a feeling of equilibrium.

It has been four weeks since Kate Thornton died. In that time, Liam has never tried to contact or find me. I suspect, for Liam, I died the day he learnt of my cancer.

The anxiety that held me prisoner and refused to allow me peace has stopped eating away at me. I no longer worry about Liam finding out about Charles and me. Instead, I am enjoying my new life as Jessica Ripley. The past cannot be changed, but my future can be moulded into whatever I want.

The bedroom door swings open and I watch Charles as he steps into the room, steaming mugs clasped in his hand. My eyes travel the length of his body, feasting on his naked form.

He is built to be admired, and I take in every glorious muscled inch of his tanned flesh, from his long, well-sculpted legs and round pert bum to the corded muscle that wraps about his abdomen. My fingers twitch, remembering how his skin feels beneath them. His thick black hair drops over his hazel eyes, obscuring them from view. My smile widens. Oh, the things I intend to do to that body. If I were a cat, I would be purring in anticipation and pleasure.

"Good morning, gorgeous." Catching me staring at him, Charles winks at me.

"Hmm… Good morning, handsome." Rearranging the pillows against the headboard, I bring myself to a sitting position, allowing the sheet to fall to my waist, revealing my breasts.

Charles' eyes darken with desire and my body shivers in response.

"Tease." Charles passes me a cup of coffee, dropping a kiss on my upturned lips.

"Oh, I'm not a tease, because once I've drunk this," I hold up the cup, "I fully intend to back it up."

Charles throws his head back and laughs. "Come here."

He raises his arm and I scurry against his side, nestling my body into his. His gentle fingers draw a circle along my upper arm as my head rests on his chest.

I sip my coffee, glad Charles never let me give up on us.

It had been hard for me to recognise that my lies were justified, especially with guilt about my fake cancer diagnosis adding to the burden. I have never been one for deceit. As I look around the room and lie here in Charles' arms, I know it was worth the personal torment I put myself through.

"Happy?" I ask. Charles has given up a lot to come live in Scotland with me, and I am aware how very different life is here.

"'Happy' doesn't cover everything I'm feeling."

"So, no regrets?"

Portree is the main town on the Isle of Skye, its natural harbour and looming cliffs creating a perfect and unspoilt place to live or visit. It's nothing like the bustle of York, and the opportunities to rise further in his career are limited here. The practice he's joined is much smaller.

City living and Charles' Piccadilly Loft apartment, with its ultra-modern design, is the polar opposite of our white-washed three-bedroom farmhouse.

The farmhouse sits on a number of acres of beautiful unspoilt grassland. On a clear day, you can see the sea as it laps at the shoreline. The rooms in the farmhouse are cosy and warm and I love each one of them. From the large inglenook, stacked high with logs ready to be thrown onto the log burner, to the country kitchen with its painted shaker cupboards. An AGA keeps the house heated and provides hot water.

Police lights, loud laughter, and partying never disturb our sleep.

The remoteness of the farmhouse is what I love the most. I never get tired of watching the birds swoop and dive or hearing them sing to each other. There's a hedgehog I've nicknamed Spike that likes to walk up to the front door and sniff round the potted plants for slugs. There is a sense of *belonging* for the first time in my life.

"No regrets. The clinic is much smaller, but the people are fantastic, and I feel that I can make a huge difference, on a more personal level."

I snuggle closer against Charles. "I love it here, and I love you." I reach across Charles, setting my empty coffee cup on the bedside table next to him. I could have used the bedside table on *my* side of the bed, but my body would have no reason to press and rub against Charles if I did.

Without asking, I take Charles' cup from him and place it next to mine. I am conscious of my breasts pressing against his hard chest, and I make sure my movements slide them over his skin. I can feel my nipples harden, and I lick my lips.

Cupping Charles' face between my hands, I straddle him.

"Thank you," I whisper, covering his lips.

Charles' hands cup my buttocks, travelling along my spine and over my chest, and I purr into his mouth.

"Now, about that teasing," I whisper in his ear.

* * *

A few hours later, we stand looking at the garden where a forgotten vegetable patch once resided. It has been invaded by weeds.

A gentle breeze caresses my skin and plays with my hair, which I have tied back in a low ponytail. A wide-brimmed hat sits on my head, keeping my face in the shade, away from the sun's glare.

There is something untameable about Scotland that has always drawn me to it. The weather, though harsh, is beautiful and forever changing – moody and dark one minute and lighting up the sky with colour the next. Nature provides us with its own wonderful show of breath-taking displays.

Life is easy. We are a small community helping each other. Though our neighbours are some miles from us, we still ensure we meet up with them from time to time. Even though we're invading Englishmen, the natives of Portree have accepted us and made us welcome.

Isolation also means the farmhouse is unprotected from the harsh weather conditions that ravish this beautiful part of the world. Charles and I spent our first week here sealing the exterior walls with weatherproof paint. There are parts of my skin that are still stained white. I remain bewildered about how it reached certain spots, though I feel Charles is to blame for that.

"So, what are you wanting to grow?" Charles rests his hands on the spade as he looks at the weed infestation.

"I'm thinking of potatoes, cabbage, carrots, onions, and cauliflowers. Oh, and maybe some beetroot. I also fancy establishing an herb garden to the right, near the window. If we put it in a window pot, it might help to discourage the slugs from eating them."

Charles stares at the small patch of ground I have marked out for a vegetable plot. "I'm not so sure you're going to fit all that in. You need to give them room to grow."

I smile at Charles. "Since we have to dig out all the weeds anyway, we could extend the patch."

"I am starting to think you're keeping me busy so I won't go looking for trouble."

I lean into Charles, giving his left bum a squeeze. "Oh, baby, I'm the only trouble you're ever going to need."

He laughs, grabbing me. "You know, if you keep this up, we're never going to get anything done."

I push myself out of his arms and place my hands on my hips. "You're right. You are just going to have to learn to control yourself."

"Me!"

I laugh at the look of astonishment on his face.

"I'm not sure I know what you're implying here."

I make an effort to look serious. "You're not, huh? Then I guess I'm just going to have to show you."

Charles grabs me and lifts me into his arms.

"You are only proving my point."

"Oh, I'll provide a *point*, all right."

I squeal as his hands move up my t-shirt. "In the vegetable patch?" I ask breathlessly.

"It'll give you something to smile about while you plant all those vegetables.

Chapter Eight

KATE

I stand looking at the red, silk, Alexandre Vauthier dress Liam has laid on the bed. It is long enough to skim my bottom and nothing more. The deep V-neckline dips down to the waist. I will need body tape to stop the edges of the fabric from exposing my breasts. There is nothing I can do about the length, other than not bend over or sit down.

The more I look at the dress, the angrier I become. It is a lovely dress, even if there isn't much of it – though I question the over two-thousand-pound price tag. My anger, however, is not at the dress, but Liam and his demand that I wear it.

With a walk-in wardrobe the size of some people's houses, I fail to understand why I am unable to choose my own outfit. Does he think me so lacking in taste that I am incapable of making such decisions? I don't believe my lack of memory has affected my capability to decide what is appropriate attire for tonight's charity function.

Fortunately, Liam's stomp in here and the choosing of the dress was the only time he visited my bedroom. In fact, since my return, other than a peck on the cheek or a guiding hand on my back, Liam has not touched me.

This pleases and worries me at the same time.

I may have lost my memory, but it doesn't mean my brain has stopped working altogether. Something doesn't stack up, and I am unable to pinpoint what that something is. At present, my lack of memory and money traps me here. My mistrust and dislike for Liam grow daily. Not that he has said or done anything to upset me. He is either in his study or at his office, so I rarely see Liam.

My life here is isolated. I am brought out and dusted off now and then to attend charity functions, such as tonight. I am nothing more than a piece of furniture to Liam, dressed to look pretty, with bouts of usefulness.

I appear to have no friends other than Jenny and, therefore, no one has visited me since I left the hospital.

Liam has informed me that my parents are dead, and I have no other living relatives. How I have managed to spend the last six years cooped up in this soulless monastery of a home with Liam without going insane, I am unsure. Life here is stagnant, and happiness is a stale feeling that holds no value.

It is seven o'clock and I am aware that, apart from showering and lathering my body in perfumed cream, I have done little in the way of getting ready. This will be the tenth charity function we've been to since I arrived at Whitegates (the residence Liam calls home, which is nothing more than a museum for collectable items). It is all tedious. Poking myself in the eye with a blunt object almost seems preferable to attending tonight's event.

What people fail to realise is that these charity functions are not about raising money as much as a way for the wealthy to show off their good fortune. Business connections are made, deals arranged, appointments confirmed. All the while, the wealthy smile and pretend to feel something for the charity on the agenda that night.

Liam walks into my room, dressed in a black Ralph Lauren Purple Label tux. The single-breasted jacket is unbuttoned, and the sides part to reveal the purple lining. "You're not ready." A look of annoyance crosses his face and his patent-leather Tom Ford Ganni shoes come to a sudden stop in the middle of the room.

"I don't think I feel up to going tonight. Why don't you go on your own, and I'll sit this one out? Just this once."

I am not sure how I will spend my time, but I find the prospect of watching a re-run of *Friends* more desirable than being paraded round a room like an expensive toy.

"You're going."

Irritation floods my system. "And I *said* I don't want to."

"Don't push me, Kate."

Ignoring the warning in Liam's voice, I sit on the bed and fold my arms. "I'm not trying to push you anywhere. I simply want to sit this one out. I'm exhausted."

"Put the dress on and get your hair and makeup fixed. I'll be back in ten minutes. By then, I want you in that dress and ready to leave."

Irritation is replaced with anger and I stand up, hands on my hips, glaring at him. "No." Tilting my head at a stubborn angle, I regard Liam. "I am not some Jack-in-the-box you can take the lid off of and expect to jump to your tune."

Before I am aware of Liam's intentions, his fist shoots out

and he punches me in the chest. Unprepared for this show of violence, the blow sends me stumbling backwards into the bedside table. My right arm takes the brunt of the fall, catching the corner of the wooden unit. The book falls to the floor and the bookmark topples from the pages. The lamp wobbles and hits the carpeted floor.

"Why are you being like this? Why can't you just be Kate?" Liam towers over me. There is no guilt on his face for what he has done, only disdain.

While his words make no sense, I do not question them. How can I *not* be Kate?

My dressing gown has parted, falling off my right shoulder, exposing the top half of my body. A large red patch is quickly turning into a bruise along my right upper arm. The pain in my chest is making it difficult to breathe, and the exposed flesh between my breasts is red. I remain where I am, though my instincts are screaming at me to run.

Liam sighs but doesn't touch me again. "You can't wear that dress now, look at you."

I refrain from mentioning that the way I look is all his fault. Shock is still telling me this isn't happening. I begin to wonder if prior to the mugging, I was planning on leaving him because I was afraid of him.

Liam marches into the walk-in wardrobe, coming back moments later with a ruby long-sleeved Stella McCartney gown. The front is cut high, and the back opens to reveal an expanse of flesh.

"This will have to do. You have ten minutes." He throws the dress on the bed and slams the door.

Hands shaking, I push myself up, sitting on the bed. My legs are like jelly, and it is as though someone has sucked out my bones. Shock is wearing off, and anger is seeping in. I can't recall a time I have ever been treated in such a callous, violent, and disrespectful way by someone I know. Of course, I have *no* memory, which explains the lack of recall. However, my sixth sense says I have never been attacked in such a way before.

One thing is clear – I have to get out of here.

When the line of violence is crossed, it will continue. All barriers are down, and there are no principles left to prevent it from happening again. I'm not sticking around long enough for a pattern of violence to form.

Right now, though, time is ticking, and I have to get dressed. There isn't enough time to throw a few items in a bag and run. When Liam says ten minutes, he means ten minutes.

Liam walks into the room. My makeup is in place and my long black hair is in a woven knot, allowing for the gap in the back of the dress to be seen. Apart from my wedding and engagement rings, I wear no jewellery. A pair of Sophia Webster gem-encrusted heels decorate my feet.

Liam nods in satisfaction. Holding the bedroom door open, he inclines his head again, indicating for me to move.

The dress floats over the floor, the slight train caressing the carpet as I step out of the bedroom. The heels tap against the marble as I make my way down the stairs.

Liam takes my elbow and I try not to flinch as his fingers graze my arm. We walk out the door to the waiting Belladonna Purple Rolls-Royce Phantom EWB and I sink into the cream leather seat.

* * *

This evening's charity event is held at Henry Henderson's, a Grade II listed country house in Colton, on the outskirts of

York. The long, pebbled drive leading up to the house is filled with cars. The wooden front doors sit open.

The Rolls-Royce comes to a smooth stop at the large stone arch at the entrance of the property.

As the car door opens, the soft sound of a string quartet playing Tchaikovsky's 'No. 1 in D Major' drifts inside.

We are a fashionable, fifteen minutes late. I don't understand the politics concerning what time is considered 'fashionably late', or what constitutes bad manners. If I turned up at the dentist fifteen minutes late, they wouldn't provide me with a warm greeting.

Liam extends his hand and, adhering to conformity and expectations, I take it as I step out of the car. My hand on his arm, we walk into the Henderson residence. I watch Liam's lips twist in distaste at the hosts' lack of greeting. The Hendersons are nowhere to be seen while their guests arrive and mingle, and it is obvious that Liam sees this lack of etiquette as a snub.

The string quartet sits within the curve of the imperial staircase. The ceiling has been adapted to provide optimum acoustics, and LED lighting has been installed to enhance the visual effect. The music vibrates through my veins and a sense of nostalgia hits me. My mind replays a scene. I'm on a blanket, looking out at the stars. A glass of champagne sits in my hand. Laughter bursts from my mouth as masculine arms pull my naked body to a set of waiting lips. A feeling of love and desire washes over me. My lips part and a sigh escapes.

"Kate." Liam's voice snaps me back to the present.

My heart becomes heavy with the sudden loss. But I place a smile on my lips as I look over at him. Those arms pulling at my naked body were not Liam's. Given Liam's need for control and the violence he has demonstrated, it is no surprise that I would look for love elsewhere.

I blink away the remaining memory and the feeling of love disappears with it.

As we begin to circulate, hungry business wannabes step forward. Compliments pour from their lips. I know from Liam's acceptance of my attire that I look stunning. I don't need empty words from strangers to confirm this. Our hands are shaken, champagne is offered, and Liam soaks up the attention. A king holding court – or, perhaps, in Liam's case, a dictator widening his sticky web of dominance.

Sipping on the champagne, I catch Jenny's eye as she wanders through the hall into the reception room. The ombre tiered gown floats about her ankles, embracing her swelling stomach.

Making my excuses, I ignore the sharp look Liam sends me and make my way over to her. "Hey, what are you doing hiding away in the corner?" A smile plays across my lips as I approach.

"Oh, I'm not hiding, just people watching. They're like vultures, aren't they?"

I look back at the crowd gathered around Liam. His sharp blue eyes assess everyone and everything, missing nothing.

"Hmm, I'm not sure that's a compliment to the vultures. I'm positive that even a scavenger has principles, unlike that lot."

"You're still not feeling any better."

I look at Jenny. "If you mean I'm still not behaving like a Stepford Wife, then yes. My memory hasn't returned, and I am still at the frustrated, snarky stage. Other than that, I am completely adorable and a pleasure to be around."

Jenny laughs. "I do like this new you."

"I'm not so sure Liam would agree."

"He's not good at accepting change, and he hates conflict."

I let the comment slide. Any conflict between me and Liam is his own doing, though I do not say this to Jenny. She's pregnant and Liam is her brother, and family is important.

Says the woman with no family.

"So, you have your bag all packed and ready?"

A large smile springs to Jenny's lips. "I've had it packed, unpacked, and repacked at least a hundred times. Dennis is finding the whole thing rather funny."

"Ah, teachers. They have a strange concept of life, and what's funny."

Jenny's husband is a professor at York University. Funnily enough, I cannot remember what he teaches.

"Now you're being mean." Jenny taps my left arm with the rim of her tall crystal glass. Orange juice swishes towards the brim.

I laugh at her reaction to my calling Dennis a teacher rather than a professor. "I just enjoy winding you two up. It's hard to say which one of you will bite first."

"OK, caught."

Liam's eyes dart in my direction. I look away and stay where I am.

"You can't ignore him forever."

"Hmmm…" I mutter, unable to think of something polite to say.

"You do that a lot when you're not happy."

Jenny is aware that her brother isn't faultless. He is cold and domineering. These things are nothing compared to the fact that Liam physically abuses his wife.

"Why do you suppose he's so controlling? I've always liked surprises, myself." The words leave my mouth before I am aware the thought was even there.

Jenny places a light hand on my right arm, and I try not to wince. Even the gentlest touch hurts.

"He's always been that way. In time, when you start to remember things, it won't seem so bad, and you'll understand him better."

There will never be a time when I will want to understand Liam. To accept the abuse.

"Perhaps." I say this for Jenny's benefit only.

People mill around us. Laughter hangs in the air, mingling with the acoustics of the string quartet.

"Why don't I have any friends?" I try to look relaxed as I ask the question. "I just find it odd that no one has come over to see me. Well, apart from you. Dennis doesn't count, he's a tagalong. Doesn't it seem rather odd to you?"

Liam shoots me another look. I won't be able to ignore him much longer.

"You have me. I'm a friend, and I come and see you."

"I didn't mean to discount you as a friend, Jenny, it's just that I never see anyone else. Where is everyone hiding? I know my parents are dead, but surely I must have *some* relatives that are alive and kicking."

"Liam hasn't told you anything?" Her eyebrows lift in surprise.

"Nope, not a thing. He's busy doing… whatever he does. But I don't think he would say anything, anyway."

"You do have an aunt."

Eagerness rolls from me. I am not alone, and the thought creates a buzz of happiness. "So, where is she? Can I see her?"

"I don't think seeing her is a good idea."

The buzz dies and confusion replaces it. "Why? Come on, give me something here. Stop being so vague."

"You asked, remember?"

I nod.

"Your aunt is in prison."

Stunned, I stare at the ceiling. The LED lights twinkle down on me and I wonder if they are laughing. "What did she do?"

"Drugs."

I sigh, resigned to having no one but Jenny and Dennis in the way of friends or family.

"When Liam met you, your aunt was trying to pimp you. You have a certain appeal, Kate, and not just to men. I've seen one or two ladies looking at you with a little more interest than what is considered appropriate. Liam finds it funny."

I don't comment, letting Jenny continue. As I remind myself, I asked the question.

"Liam likes the idea of rescuing you. A bit like Richard Gere in *Pretty Woman*."

I shake my head, not seeing the similarity. Despite what Jenny has said, I do not believe Liam's gallantry has anything to do with rescuing me from my aunt. I believe it has more to do with him wanting to acquire me for himself. At the moment, other than being a trophy wife, I am not seeing much gain for me.

"Sorry," Jenny mutters at my silence.

"No, don't worry, I asked."

Liam has manoeuvred himself within the group of people gathered around him, so he is looking directly at me. I acknowledge that my time with Jenny has reached its limit.

Inclining my head in Liam's direction, I sigh. "I believe I've loitered here too long."

Jenny smiles. "Look, before you scat, how do you fancy meeting for lunch tomorrow? I still have a few things I need to get before this little one is born. I've only got a couple of months to go and, with it being my first, I don't want to leave things until the last minute."

"I have to ask what you could still need. I've seen the nursery and the rest. That baby already has more than it needs. However, lunch sounds great."

As I turn to go, I look back at Jenny. "By the way, I have not failed to notice that, with Dennis lecturing, you're on the lookout for another packhorse to carry your bags."

"When did you become such a pessimist, Kate?"

"When I saw you shop." She giggles.

"I'll ring you tomorrow morning to firm everything up."

I gave Jenny a quick salute as I walk over to Liam.

Chapter Nine

LIAM

My annoyance at Kate increases as she talks to Jenny. I know she has seen me watching her and has chosen to ignore me. Her role here is to mingle at my side and look glamorous. At present, she has achieved only one of her required duties.

There is an air of confidence about her that my Kate never possessed. While it has a certain appeal, I expect full compliance from her at all times, which I am not receiving. The dress she's wearing accentuates her slim figure. It moulds to her body, hugging her waist and caressing her breasts and thighs. The red brings out the richness of her caramel skin. Men openly stare at her, desire lighting their eyes.

The air of vulnerability that wrapped itself around my Kate is missing. This new Kate is stubborn and unyielding. She leaves no room for acceptance. I am aware that I will need to act on it. Stamp out her stubbornness. It is why I have taken out an insurance policy. If she will not yield to my demands, I have something that will force her into submission.

Kate winces as Jenny touches her right arm. It is the first time I have ever hit Kate. In actual fact, I *still* have never hit Kate. The person I hit is Kate's identical twin sister, Chrissie. Even though it is difficult to accept my flaws, I do, and so I admit I was not prepared for Chrissie's defiance. My poise slipped and I hit her. Weakness laughed and my control evaporated. At that moment, I became as pitiful as Pete Townsend.

I will never allow her to damage me in that way again. Chrissie has to go. To do that, I will need to break her until all that is left is my Kate. I will do whatever it takes. Chrissie will not ruin all my careful planning, or me.

Strangely, I thought the amnesia was the weak part in my plan. It never occurred to me that Chrissie wouldn't be as submissive as my Kate. They are identical twins, after all, carbon copies of each other. However, it appears that even though they are genetically the same, their personalities are quite different. Chrissie needs to understand that she is my Kate now, and as such, she has to behave like my Kate. There is no room for negotiation.

The tinkling of Kate's laughter rises above the noise of the quartet, like the chime of soft bells. Enticing and enchanting.

Kate and Jenny are getting on better than ever. It is just as well that I have been careful with the information surrounding Kate's upbringing and family life. While Jenny knows about the aunt and drugs, she does not know about the sister, and my Kate never mentioned it to anyone. A little too late, I find her actions interesting. Why the secrecy?

I arch a brow at Kate and her smile dies on her lips. She leans into Jenny before walking over to me. The confident tap of her heels tells me Chrissie is still alive and well inside my Kate. If she expects me to feel guilt or remorse for hitting her, she will be disappointed. I cannot recall a time that I have felt or harboured any feeling of regret for something I have done. Violence isn't what I am about, but if needs be, I can commit to it.

"Kate is looking particularly lovely tonight." Henry Henderson stands at my side and I wonder where the fat slug has been hiding the last hour.

Henry Henderson is self-made money. They are the worst. There is no refinement to be found in this type of person. If only the Hendersons had stayed in the gutter where they belonged, I would not be forced to be here.

The Henderson's are loud and brash, throwing money around to prove their worth. Money speaks quietly. It is power, not an ornament to dangle in everyone's faces. Before the year is up, I will bankrupt Henry Henderson and put him back in the gutter where he belongs.

Nevertheless, I smile at Henry. Diplomacy is what life is about, and until our deal is signed, I will partake in this well-oiled game.

"Henry, you have outdone yourself tonight," I lie.

Henry beams as Kate arrives at my side. I place a hand on her back, using more pressure than required, in a subtle declaration of dominance.

"Kate, I was just saying to Liam how lovely you look tonight."

Henry takes Kate's delicate hand between his chubby ones and places his grubby lips on the back of it. The man really doesn't have any redeeming qualities.

Henry is in his early thirties. The extra weight he carries not only reduces his life expectancy... it adds another ten years to his age. Sweat lines the young man's forehead and his jowls wobble as he speaks.

I am undecided what he hopes to achieve by wearing a colour-block Burberry tuxedo. While the label denotes quality, Henry manages to make the black-and-white jacket appear cheap.

Kate smiles as she takes back her hand. "Why, Henry, you are too gracious."

Henry chuckles, ogling her. "The auction is due to start any minute, and I was wondering if Kate would care to help me out?"

Naturally, it is my approval Henry seeks. Not even he is stupid enough to think it's Kate choice.

"Where is Jane?" I refrain from stating the obvious – though, given that it is Henry I am speaking to, perhaps I should have told him it is poor etiquette and somewhat vulgar to expect a guest to 'help out'.

Jane is Henry's wife. She is as skinny as Henry is fat. Despite all her cosmetic surgery, her body and face remain plain and forgettable. Jane is loud and her squeaky voice grates.

"She's putting little Jamie to bed."

"Ah…" I nod, and my consent is granted.

Kate has not been with me long enough to understand my subtle agreement to Henry's use of her. Henry, however, beams like a lighthouse.

The world is not a blessed place. Jamie Henderson is eight and is the reason for tonight's charity event. The boy was born with a congenital heart condition. Pulmonary atresia. It affects the valve that lets blood out of the heart to travel to the lungs. Instead of opening and closing, a solid tissue forms, preventing the flow of blood. It is a worthwhile cause, yet it is secondary to the amount of business being conducted.

Jamie is loud like his mother and has the misfortune of having Henry's appetite for unhealthy foods. I do not see a future for the boy, especially when his father can no longer pay for his private treatment.

"It will be my pleasure." Kate steps forward, linking her arm with Henry's.

"Perfect, perfect." Henry guides Kate towards the far room, where the auction is due to take place.

The theme of tonight's auction is fine wine. Most people in this room have contributed. And now, we get the opportunity to buy it back at an inflated price.

The quartet comes to a stop and Henry's voice sounds through the speakers. Like mindless sheep, we are herded into the temporary auction room. The normal furnishings have been removed, replaced with row upon row of metal chairs. I loiter at the back so I can look at the gathering crowd. Kate stands on the temporary stage. There was a grace about my Kate that I always admired. Chrissie has the same commanding presence.

With a burst of activity, the auction begins. Bottle after bottle is paraded in front of us. Tammy Sinclair jumps up from her seat and raises her paddle, increasing her bid to twenty thousand pounds. Her large breasts bob about, threatening to break free of the skimpy red fabric of her low-cut dress. Tammy is our resident alcoholic. She will drink anything.

Her husband, Jeremy, grabs her arm and pulls her back to her chair. Angry whisperings can soon be heard over the beating of the wooden hammer.

Tammy slides down in her seat, sulking like a toddler. Jeremy is always threatening to divorce her. He won't, of course, as the money is Tammy's. Instead, Jeremy waits for nature to takes its course and for liver disease to claim his wife. It is a long, drawn-out process. Jeremy would be better off if he locked Tammy in a well-stocked wine cellar.

Paula Clarkson sniggers into the ear of her latest husband. At sixty-seven, Paula is pumped full of enough Botox to stop any type of emotion from ever crossing her face again. Paula's first husband, the one whose money she is now spending, died of a heart attack five years into their marriage. At thirty-two, Paula was a stunning widow. She has spent the following thirty-five years taking up with any young man who is willing and able.

Paula, however, is old money, and with it comes style and class. The simple black Alexander McQueen dress hugs her trim figure. The black lace along the arms and back add to the glamorous feel of the gown. The plastic surgeons and health farms make sure Paula keeps her thirty-two-year-old shape and looks.

Paula's eyes linger on Kate and even from this distance, I notice her jealousy. Paula has always disliked Kate's natural beauty. I smile because I like to see envy for what is mine.

Paula's current husband, John Templeton, is in his late twenties. His sky-blue eyes lock onto Kate's body as she moves about the stage.

Something stirs within me, something I haven't felt in a long time. Desire for the woman I have made mine. It is unexpected, and I begin to wonder if a visit to her bedroom is in order tonight.

Kate catches me watching her, and the sparkle in her eyes dies.

Irritation replaces desire. It is as well. I can do without the emotional entanglement.

With the last bottle sold, I walk forward to reclaim my

bottle of 1996 Dom Perignon Rose Gold Methuselah, which cost me fifty thousand pounds. The money is currently being wired over to the charity.

Kate is standing at my side as Henry's wife makes her appearance. Jane is dressed in Patricia Bonaldi. The nude lining stops high on her thighs, leaving the transparent mesh and decorative embellishment to shimmer down her legs. The front of the dress plunges to her waist, and triangles of flesh appear where the fabric has been cut to narrow in the waist. Jane manages to make the five-thousand-three-hundred-fifty-pound dress look like high-street trash. I know the price because I almost bought it from Harrods for Kate, rather than the Stella McCartney she is wearing.

"Thanks for looking after things while I put Jamie to bed. He has such terrible trouble getting off to sleep. I think it's from all the surgery he had when he was a baby." Jane's gratefulness is as shallow as the space between her tits.

Kate smiles. "It was a pleasure."

Tony Carlton stands behind Jane. The tuxedo he is wearing enhances his dark brooding looks, chiselled features, and strong jawline. His latest conquest hangs off his arm, a dreamy look on her face as she stares at him.

Tony coughs. "The pleasure was all ours, I assure you."

Jane's back stiffens at Tony's words. "Tony. I didn't see you, loitering back there like a naughty boy."

"I wasn't loitering, Jane, just appreciating the view." He winks at Kate.

Jane's cheeks redden. The green beading on her dress matches the jealous spark in her eyes as they sweep over Kate.

"Women aren't baubles to be leered at." Jane reprimands Tony.

She is known for her fiery temper and has taken a swing

at her guests in the past. While her hair is red, it is not her natural colour, so I cannot put her barbaric nature down to the pigmentation of her hair. I blame her lower-class background.

"Don't worry, Jane, it wasn't you I was leering at."

The woman dangling off Tony's arm begins to pout.

While I find Jane and Tony's exchange amusing, I move Kate into the crook of my arm. I do this not to protect her, though I am aware it looks that way, but to remind them that Kate is mine.

"You're a lucky man, Liam."

I nod at Tony in agreement. "Indeed, I am. Now, if you will excuse us." I turn to Jane. "It has been a lovely evening, thank you for the invitation."

"Yes… Yes… Simply splendid," Henry stutters as the quartet begins packing up.

I air-kiss Jane's cheeks. "I will arrange for the champagne to be collected later."

Taking Kate's arm, I steer her out of the room before Tony attempts to kiss her. Neither of us speak as we settle into the waiting Rolls-Royce.

The journey to Whitegates is quiet, and I am content to allow the silence to continue. I need time to work out how I am going to get rid of Chrissie.

Chapter Ten

LIAM

The tapping of Kate's heels on the marble stairs follows me into the study. Switching on the light by my desk, I leave the rest of the room in shadow. The deep-red walls add to the darkness, and the small window doesn't allow for the moonlight to penetrate.

The cool temperature in the room keeps the Rembrandt on the back wall protected, as does the lack of light. The distinct strokes of the brushwork are hidden by the dimness. I do not admire the painting, nor the workmanship. It is enough that it is mine, and others want it. That is where true satisfaction lies.

A red light flashes on the answering machine sitting on the Regency mahogany desk. It is a habit of mine to divert my mobile to my office line. Taking calls during a charity function is unrefined and shows a lack of breeding.

With a sigh, I slide the ox-blood Duke Chesterfield office chair back and sit down, pressing the button on the machine.

Henry Henderson's booming voice filters through the speaker. "Liam, sorry to ring you so late."

Having just left his property, I find the apology stale. Henry knows I will be up.

"Paula has just been saying that she saw Kate at a cancer clinic a month or so ago, and, well, Jane and I, we wanted to pass on our concern and let you know we are here for you and Kate."

Jane's voice echoes in the background, bleating words of comfort she doesn't mean.

"Of course, Paula could have gotten it wrong. She said she was in a state because her uncle had been taken in the very same day. She said she wouldn't have thought much of it, but Kate was carrying an overnight bag and, well, why would she need a bag if she was just visiting someone?

"Well, anyway, as I said, Jane and I are here for you. I just want to let you know. It's dreadful news, dreadful, Kate, poor Kate. Call me if you want to reschedule our appointment on Monday."

Jane is still squeaking in the background as the line goes dead.

I continue staring at the answering machine for a long time after Henry's words have disappeared. My hands ball and I want to smash the machine into tiny pieces. The control I have woven around my emotions prevents me from taking action.

How dare Henry Henderson pretend to try and understand how I am feeling?

I take a deep breath, focusing on the problem. Panicking solves nothing. Though my heart increases its tempo, I exhibit no other signs of tension.

Apart from Charles, no one knows about Kate's cancer. I will ensure Paula stops her gossiping and remind her who assisted her into widowerhood at thirty-two. By the time I finish with Paula, she will understand my distaste when it comes to these matters. Obviously, some damage has already been done, which she will have to undo. If she appears foolish while cleaning up her mess, she has only her mouth and lack of cognitive processing to blame.

The fact remains that, at the time of Kate's visit to the hospice, new Kate (Chrissie) was lying unconscious in the hospital after a vicious and unwarranted attack. Charles was long gone, and I hadn't heard from him since he left for Scotland. Having no intention of keeping in contact with him, I never asked for his new address. His mobile number is no longer in my list of contacts.

Charles! My foolishness crashes down on me as my own cognitive processing steps up a gear.

Records of Kate's cancer, her test results and scans, will still be held at the clinic Charles worked at. I berate myself for not thinking about this earlier. My focus at the time had been on finding an answer to the issue around my wife's death. That solved, I had stupidly allowed myself to relax. However, this problem is easier to solve than the complexity of replacing my dead wife with her twin sister.

My sloppiness does nothing to dispel my rising anger.

Taking my mobile from the inside pocket of my jacket, I select Pete's number. My fingers beat against the ox-blood leather on the desk as impatience crawls along my spine.

"H-Hello?" Pete's sleepy voice sounds down the line.

"You need to get dressed. I have a job for you."

There is a rustling of fabric as Pete moves.

"At four in the morning?"

I am an educated man. I learnt to tell time while at primary school. My memory is still intact, and dementia has not set in. Given this, I do not appreciate Pete's need to state the obvious.

"I see no relevance in what time of day it is. There is a job to be done, and you will do it."

"At four in the morning?"

"Get over your fixation with the bloody time. We have a problem and you are going to fix it."

"I fixed the last one, my debt is paid."

The grip on my mobile tightens. "Don't." My threat buzzes down the phone. Pete relinquished any freedom he possessed when he blundered his way through completing Kate's file.

"What do you need me to do?"

I never informed Pete of the reason I needed Chrissie. "My wife, Kate, had terminal cancer..."

"Oh, I'm sorry to hear that."

"Don't interrupt," I snap. I have no use for Pete's sympathy.

Pete mutters his apology.

"It is why I needed her sister, Chrissie. I take it you remember her?"

"Yes."

"Good. I need you to destroy the files at the oncology unit Kate attended."

My fingers cease drumming and my heart returns to its natural rhythm as I give Pete the clinic's details.

"Make sure you are thorough. I want no trace left, paper or electronic. When you have finished at York Hospital, you will pay a visit to the hospice Kate went to, and make sure any personal files and references to her stay are removed. Do you understand?"

"Yes, Mr. Thornton."

"And, Pete, I want this done straight away. Ring me when it's done. I am not bothered what time it is."

"Yes, Mr. Thornton."

I terminate the call. Later, I will ring Henry. Once I've sorted out Paula.

Chapter Eleven

KATE

Kicking off my trainers, I stop the running app and begin stretching on the manicured lawn with a number of yoga positions. Music blares through the cordless headphones as I move my body from Tadasana into Utthita Parsvakonasana.

The run did nothing to calm my anger at Liam, or at myself. Normally, I run around ten kilometres a day. It clears my head of the constant pounding and frustration over my lack of memory. This morning is different. My timing is off. My legs feel heavy, my feet sluggish, and my pace slow. Therefore, I could only squeeze in six kilometres before I needed to stop so I'll have time to get ready for lunch with Jenny.

A large bruise stains my right arm, forcing me to strap my phone onto my left. The strap is an uncomfortable reminder of what Liam has done, and what I have allowed to happen to me.

There is no reasoning with self-blame, it is as irrational as it is complex. With no memory, no money, and no friends or family (other than Jenny and Dennis), I am stuck here at Whitegates with Liam. The police are limited in what they can do, and Liam has many friends. I take that back. My complaint to Jenny that I have no friends also rings true for Liam. He doesn't have *friends*, only business associates – not that I believe he feels his lack of friendships the same way I do.

Friends talk about their problems, and I am betting Liam doesn't want anyone to know what our relationship is really like. This thought clears up my confusion about my no-friends status, especially because I feel like I am a social person.

Screaming out my frustration is appealing, but however emotionally satisfying it would be, I am not prepared to let Liam know how much he has affected me. Instead, I pick up my trainers and socks and make my way into the house to get washed and changed.

Turning on the shower, water spills over my head and body, massaging my skin. Time passes as I stand under the faucet, and my brain niggles at me to start getting clean. Motivation is hard to find, but I do.

The bruise on my chest looks angry, as does the one on my arm. My reaction to Liam's abuse signals that this is the first time I have experienced it. Though I have no physical memory to support this, I will trust my instincts while maintaining as much distance from Liam as possible. I feel that my hate for Liam is greater than any I have felt in my life. Again, I will trust my inner voice on this.

My hands clench into fists at my sides, calling for release. Liam's face would be a good, if impossible, target.

As it isn't going to happen, I spread out my fingers, releasing them from the tight balls they have formed.

If Liam thinks by hitting me, I will become more compliant to his demands, he is wrong. The bruises fire my temper and I tell myself Liam can stick his charity events up his arse. I am not his bauble to dangle off his arm, smiling and pretending we are the perfect happy couple. Once I work out how I can leave this place and still afford to live, dust will be the only thing lingering at his side.

My mood is still darkening as I walk into the wardrobe to see what designer outfit will adorn my body today. It is already warm outside, and though a sleeveless top and shorts would fit the weather, there is the problem of covering my bruises. I don't want Jenny asking questions.

Fifteen minutes later, I decide to wear a floral silk Chloé dress with dusky tones. The wide sleeves fall to my hands, and the peplum hem sits two inches above my knees. I am not one for high necklines, but the square-cut design rests above my collarbone, covering the bruise on my chest. Fastening the matching belt, I reach for a pair of two-and-half inch (I wouldn't want to forget about the half inch) sandals. My make-up is light, and my hair falls loose about my waist. Grabbing a two-tone Burberry shoulder bag, I walk into the bedroom to collect my lipstick.

As I open the bag to drop in the lipstick, I become aware of a problem. I have no money or cards. My eyes close and I take a laboured breath. What use does a woman with amnesia require with a credit card? Even if I had one, I wouldn't know the PIN. Contactless is not going to get me a place to stay and food on the table. Nor will it by lunch for Jenny and I.

There is only one solution to my problem. I need to ask Liam for a handout. How I am going to broach the subject is an interesting quandary. *"Hi, hun, fancy giving me some money? How much? Oh, I don't know, a few hundred, so I can hole up somewhere as far away from you as possible?"* I have a feeling that won't work, though it is a pleasing thought.

My heels click on the floor as I walk towards the office door. I want to knock my head against it. I refrain and use my hand.

"Yes?" Liam's clipped voice sounds through the thick wood.

Reminding myself I am capable of doing this, I take a deep breath as I press down on the handle and walk inside.

There is an air of gloom about the place. The dark-red walls and small window allow little light to enter, and the large dark furniture adds to the glumness.

"I'm going to meet Jenny in York for some pre-baby shopping."

Liam's eyes sweep over my body, taking in my dress – the long sleeves and high neckline meets his approval and he nods in satisfaction.

I wonder how much money I would make if I sold tickets to punch him. Perhaps I should suggest as a theme for the next charity function.

Liam sits back in his chair. Placing his fingers together, he stares at me.

"I need some money."

He doesn't blink.

"To pay for lunch."

A smile touches his lips. "Of course."

I remain glued to the mahogany floor as Liam walks over to the far wall and reveals a safe. The room, despite its enormous size, makes me feel claustrophobic.

The mahogany desk is littered with paperwork. I assume

it is the contract he wants Henry to sign. A Persian rug covers the floor at the rear of the room, where two high-back Queen Anne chairs sit facing each other beneath a Rembrandt. This is Liam's domain, and I am conscious I don't belong.

The safe door clicks shut, and Liam throws a wad of cash onto his desk as he sits down.

I stare at the cash, wondering if there will be enough for me to leave and not come back. The bundle of twenties appears sufficient, at least for lunch.

"Jake Junior is taking the Aston Martin in for a service. He'll drop you off in town. You can get a taxi back."

I nod, picking up the notes. The impulse to start counting the cash is powerful, but I refrain, promising myself I will count it once I am away from Liam's scrutinizing gaze.

Liam's voice stops me as I reach the door. "Henry Henderson will be coming over on Monday. You are required to make yourself available. He will be bringing Jane and that kid of his with him."

My fingers tighten around the money. "Of course."

As the door closes, I lean against it. Opening my hand, I stare down at the cash and start counting. Five hundred pounds sits in the palm of my hand. It's a lot of money for lunch, but I am not going to complain. I smile. It's enough to give me a chance to distance myself from Liam and form a plan. But first I will meet with Jenny. It's too late for me to cancel on her now.

This time as I walk across the marble floor, my sandals beat out a happy tune. I close the front door knowing I won't be back. Giddiness bubbles up and I place the Tom Ford sunglasses over my eyes as I walk over to the Aston Martin.

Jake Junior is already sitting in the car. The smile on his face says this is the stuff his dreams are made of. He has yet to notice my approach, and I stand watching him as he pretends to adjust a bow tie. Pulling at the sleeves of his clean blue overalls as though tugging on the sleeves of a tux, he checks himself out in the mirror. Not happy with what he sees, he rakes his hair back from his face, giving himself a side parting. With his red hair and wiry frame, Junior is no Sean Connery, but in his mind, at this moment, as he sits in the driver's seat of the Aston Martin, he is the best James Bond there has ever been.

Junior catches me watching him and blushes. His smile remains as he jumps out of the car and opens the passenger door for me. I smile back at him, amusement sparkling in the depths of my emerald eyes. It is the first time in a long time I have forgotten my own problems and allowed someone else's happiness to wash over me.

"Mrs. Thornton," Jake Junior acknowledges me as he closes the car door and races round to the driver's side.

"Where would you like dropping off?" he asks, giving the steering wheel a loving pat.

"If you drop me outside the Minster, that will be fine." My smile broadens. "But, before you do, why don't you take her for a spin down by the old Harrison estate? The place is empty and the road leading up to it is straight. Maybe you'd like to open up the engine and really see what she can do?"

Junior's eyes light up. We both know Liam would have a heart attack if he knew we were taking this beauty out for a joyride. However, for tax purposes, the logbook is in my name, which means I own the car. While this information might have me driving the car into the nearest garage and selling it, I don't have access to my bank, or the logbook.

Junior hesitates.

"Go for it, Jake Junior. You may never get another

opportunity."

His head bobs and the engine rumbles to life. The car moves sedately down the drive. If Liam is watching, he will think his instructions are being adhered to. The thought of our small deception makes me feel smug.

Freedom, in the true meaning of the word, is something that rarely exists. Demands are made upon us that remove free choice. Better known as responsibility. Yet, as the Aston Martin grumbles along the road and the scenery flashes past, I taste freedom. Free of self-doubt, of shame and anger. Liam's ownership cannot touch me here. For twenty minutes, I purr with the car's engine in happiness.

Like most things, the moment passes too quick. Before I am ready, Junior pulls the car to a stop outside the York Minster.

Jumping out, he opens my door. "Thank you, Mrs. Thornton."

"I think I should be the one saying thank you. That was some driving, back there."

Junior beams, and I know that, for him, today will live on long after the moment has passed.

Walking down High Petergate, I make my way to meet Jenny. By the time I get there, Jenny already has several shopping bags. I have arrived at the designated time.

I look at the bulging bags. "What time did you start?"

"Dennis dropped me off on his way to work. I'm too fat to drive. The steering wheel keeps getting in the way of my bump."

"Didn't you think of adjusting the steering-wheel column?"

Jenny laughs, lifting her bags. "What? And miss out on getting in extra shopping time?"

I shake my head at her. "Here, give me your bags. This carthorse needs something to carry."

"So, where to now?" I ask as I rearrange them.

"Why don't we go for a drink? I could do with sitting down for a bit. My feet are beginning to swell." Jenny loops her arm through mine. "Come, let's see if we can get a table at the Judges' Lodgings."

The Judges' Lodgings earned its name back in 1806, when it provided accommodation for visiting judges due to sit in the Assize Courts.

Our progress is slow due to the mass of tourists milling down the street. Jenny is tiring quickly. As we turn right onto Lendal, the Grade II listed Georgian townhouse comes into view. The hotel-cum-pub-and-restaurant is a popular venue for the residents of York, and most of the tables in the courtyard are already taken. I find us a spot in the shade and, placing the shopping bags on the ground, I pull out a chair for Jenny.

"Oh great, I need to pee." Jenny pushes herself out of the metal chair. "What do you want to drink? I'll get the order in on my way to the bathroom."

I put my purse away. "I'll have a latte, thanks."

Jenny nods, waddling to the pub's entrance.

People watching, I am finding, is one of my favourite pastimes. I sit back and relax. My eyes fall on a man in his early thirties. His short black hair is starting to turn grey at the sides, giving him a dash of ruggedness.

Lines appear on my forehead. There is something familiar about him. I move the chair to get a better look. My heart flips as I stare at him.

At six-foot-two, he towers above me. The thick muscles on his legs and arms highlight his sporty nature. As a personal trainer, he uses his sculpted physique to motivate his clients in achieving their goals. I don't question how I know he is a personal trainer. I just accept it.

The attraction I feel towards this man is staggering. My body aches to feel his touch. To be wrapped in those tanned arms. His confident swagger, his jeans which pull and stretch across his bum and thighs cause my heat to beat faster and desire to rise.

I am transported back in time, laying on a blanket beneath the stars, champagne glass in hand, my heart full of love for the man next to me. His arms, those tanned arms that swing at his sides as he walks down Lendal, are the ones from my vision at Henry Henderson's charity event.

A child cries at his side and he bends down, hugging her before swinging her onto his shoulders. Her long black hair cascades down her back.

My heart beats in recognition. This is *my* child, *my* husband. I can't explain how I know this. I just do. Unconsciously, I twist the rings on my left hand as the door to my memories open and floods my brain and body with emotion. Confusion. I'm questioning what I know to be right. The wedding album Liam brought to the hospital… That bride is me. There can be no conspiracy going on. Not even Liam can influence everyone I have met since coming out of the hospital. Everyone has recognised me as Kate.

Kate… I pause. The name has never suited me. And then it hits me. My name is *Chrissie*. Kate is my identical twin sister. Oh, God. My hands tremble as they rest on the table and the full impact of what Liam has done hits me. I care little for his motivations. I only feel the effects his actions have on me.

Forgetting about Jenny, I stand up, needing to leave here, to be with Simon and my daughter, Imogen. I'll destroy Liam for what he has done to me, to Simon and Imogen. Somehow, I will show him he can't drag me into his life without consequences. I will tear his well-ordered world to pieces.

Liam's words echo round my head. *"Why can't you be Kate?"* The answer is clear: I'm not Kate.

What have you done, Liam? Has he struck Kate and killed her? Fear sends a cold shiver down my spine. It is easy to see how I make the perfect replacement for my sister. No one would suspect a thing. Any difference in personality is easily explained away by my amnesia. *I'll give you amnesia, you sneaky bastard!* I will go to the police, get him locked up for this. He won't be able to buy his way out.

I have been such a fool. I should have known better. All my instincts have been screaming at me that things weren't right, that I was missing something. My hands clench and I knock the chair over as I stand and begin weaving my way through the tables to Simon.

"Kate! Kate!" Jenny's screams fill the courtyard.

I stop, turning around.

She waddles at speed towards me. Her dress is wet. "My water broke." Her eyes are wide with panic.

There is a moment's hesitation when all I want to do is run. Run to Simon and throw my arms round his neck. My head swings back to find him gone. I close my eyes. We will be together soon. Right now, I have to take care of Jenny.

"Don't panic."

The look on Jenny's face tells me she thinks I am insane.

It is a stupid thing to say to someone in the midst of labour, two months early.

"Breathe." Snaking an arm round her neck, I start demonstrating slow, deep, even breaths.

"Oh, God, it's happening, Kate, I'm going to have my

baby." Panic grips her again. "I can't have my baby here."

"You're not going to. The hospital isn't that far from here. I'll get a taxi or something." I look around, aware we aren't going to make it to the nearest taxi rank, and there is no way Jenny will be able to walk to the hospital.

The first contraction hits her. This baby is coming.

A man walks over to us. "My car's parked across the road. Do you want me to take you to the hospital?"

"Thanks, that would be great." We don't really have a lot of choice. Jenny's baby isn't going to wait.

I wrap an arm around Jenny as she huffs next to me. The man picks up the shopping bags and guides us over to his car, opening the back door.

"My wife had our first child in the supermarket, in the frozen veg isle. I know what it's like."

Jenny lets out a breath and I look at my watch, timing the contractions as we slowly make our way onto Station Road. Our driver rolls down his car windows, pressing his horn and turning on his hazard lights.

Leaning out the window, he shouts at the line of traffic, "Baby coming! Come on, let me through!"

A policeman on a motorbike pulls up alongside us, lights flashing, and Jenny screams. I hope her scream is panic and not another contraction.

"Don't worry, ladies, the cavalry's here," the stranger chuckles. He points in the back. "Baby comin'!"

The policeman looks into the back of the car.

Next to me, Jenny huffs as I try to get her breathing back on track.

The policeman nods. "Follow me." And, like the Red Sea parted for Moses, so the traffic parts for us. Our car speeds forward, following the flashing police lights.

Grabbing my phone, I ring Dennis. "Jenny's water broke and we're on our way to the hospital."

I hang up without giving him a chance to say anything. There is no time to enter into a conversation.

"You're doing really well, Jenny. We're nearly there."

The hospital looms before us and, with a squeal of tyres, we enter the grounds.

Alerted by the policeman, hospital staff are waiting outside, ready to receive Jenny.

Jenny's hand grips mine. "Don't leave me, Kate."

"Relax. I'm here for the long haul."

My sandals clack on the tiles. I keep a tight hold on Jenny's hand as we make our way into the hospital.

Chapter Twelve

JESSICA

I stare at the white stick in my hand. The words on the tiny screen confirm that I am pregnant. Dropping the pregnancy-test stick into the basket near the toilet, I listen to it clink against the other six sticks. Each one has provided the same result. I am definitely pregnant. After taking seven tests, I am satisfied. Perhaps it is excessive to take the test seven times before believing the information is correct. I don't care.

Giddy with excitement, I smooth down my pale-blue cotton summer dress and step out of the bathroom.

Dreams are heady things when they come true. I am having Charles' baby. This makes me giggle as I jump about on the landing, unable to stand still. My bubble of happiness continues as I float downstairs, my bare feet sinking into the carpet. *Get a grip,* I tell myself as I enter the kitchen. There is a lot to do before Charles gets home. I want the moment I tell him about our baby to be special, and special takes time to prepare.

Reaching for the cookbook sitting on the kitchen unit, I thumb through the pages for inspiration. Charles isn't a fancy-food man, and I decide to go traditional. Happy with my decision, I hum as I get out the ingredients.

Flour coats the kitchen surfaces and a rolling pin sits next to the pastry as the KitchenAid binds the cake mixture together. I chop and dice vegetables and my bubble of happiness continues growing as the food cooks.

Ten minutes before Charles is due home, I slip into the bedroom and take out a pair of little white booties I bought a few months back. At the time, it seemed as if I was tempting fate. I squeal with delight as I lift them out of the clear plastic box, and I am glad I bought them.

The front door clicks, and I run into the kitchen, hiding the booties as Charles walks in.

"Something smells good," Charles calls as he walks into the kitchen.

His eyes lock on the steak pie I've placed on the heatproof mat. "Hmmm, this looks great."

Laughing, I wink at him. "If you think this is good, you should see what I've got planned for dessert."

Charles laughs as he snakes his arms around my waist, pulling me to him, his lips kissing my neck. "Why don't we have dessert first?"

Shaking my head, I move out of his arms, placing my hands flat against his chest, stopping him from kissing me. "You know dessert is always best saved until last. Besides, trust me when I say you're going to need the energy this meal will provide."

"Tease."

"Definitely. Now, go get yourself changed into something more comfortable. Food's up in ten minutes."

A wicked glint appears in his eyes. "Something more comfortable, hmmmm… I think I can manage that."

He pulls at his tie as he walks out the room.

Shaking my head at him, I start setting the table. Humming to myself, I give the table another once-over before setting down the pie.

My jaw drops as Charles walks in and leans against the door frame.

He smiles at my reaction. "Will this do?"

I simply nod, my eyes raking his naked body.

"You did say *comfortable*."

Yes, I did.

"Let's just hope you don't drop any gravy on your…" I wave my hand at him. "Well, just be careful."

He throws his head back and laughs at me. Walking into the room, he grabs me and his hands roam over my body.

A moan escapes my lips and desire heats my blood. Breathless, I tear my lips from his.

"Stop it, or tea's going to get cold."

"I like cold pie."

I point at the chair by the table. "Sit, Romeo."

"Spoilsport."

"You know what they say about anticipation."

His stomach rumbles.

"See?"

Charles smiles as his eyes slide over the food on the table. "This looks great, Jess."

I beam at the compliment.

"Thank you." Reaching for the pie, I cut off a good-size chunk for Charles.

"So, what did I do to earn this?"

Oh, baby, you have no idea. "I want to spoil my man."

"I like the sound of that."

"So do I." Leaning forward, I kiss him.

Charles tucks into the food on his plate and I watch him as I eat, my bubble of happiness getting bigger and bigger.

"That was delicious." Charles wipes his mouth with a napkin.

"I'm glad you liked it." Picking up his plate, my heart begins pounding against my chest.

Taking the white booties out of the drawer, I hide them behind my back.

"Close your eyes."

Charles wiggles an eyebrow at me as he does what he's told.

I place the little booties in front of him and bend down, my mouth close to his ear.

"This is what you did," I whisper. "Open your eyes."

Charles' eyes fly open and I cock my head at the table. He looks down and sees the booties. His mouth curves into the biggest smile I have ever seen, and I feel like I am going to burst with happiness. Imprinting this moment on my brain, I swear to never forget the look of sheer joy and wonder on his face.

"This is…. This…is… It's *wonderful.*" Charles grabs me and I fall into his lap with a shriek of delight.

"Happy?" I ask, needing him to vocalise his feelings. Six years with Liam have left me needing reassurance, and while I am aware of my insecurities, I am unable to stop them from surfacing when my emotions run high.

Charles shakes his head. "No. I'm more than happy." His lips meet mine. "You're wonderful, Jess."

"It was a joint effort."

Charles swings me in the air as he stands up. "I love you."

My heart flips. "I love you too."

Walking out of the kitchen, Charles carries me to the stairs.

"What about dessert?" I ask.

"I'm just about to have it."

"You'd better be careful, this dessert bites back," I warn him.

Charles laughs. "I'm counting on it."

I giggle against his shoulder.

Chapter Thirteen

LIAM

Something is wrong.

This feeling persists as I sit staring at the Rembrandt. Kate has rejected all my calls. Thanks to Dennis' call enquiring if I required a lift to the hospital, I know Kate is there with Jenny. I am perplexed as to why he thinks I would need to attend such matters. Babies are born all the time, though I did not mention this to Dennis. I simply informed him that my business commitments prevented me from doing so.

Kate was with Jenny during the birth and remained with her until Dennis arrived. I am informed of this via text (Dennis again). So why is Kate still not picking up?

Patience is not a virtue I have cultivated in myself, and my fingers drum an angry beat against the leather on the mahogany desk. Control bites at my nerves, demanding that I wait for Pete's call. Time is becoming my tormentor as it ticks a slow and continuous reminder of its passing.

Trust is another virtue I am lacking. The mahogany Wag-staff bell-chiming verge-bracket clock from the 1800s sings out the passing of another fifteen minutes. Plan B is looking increasingly likely. It not an action I wish to take, as killing Kate renders all my previous actions unnecessary.

The clock chimes and another fifteen minutes have passed.

Turning the key, I open the drawer on my left and remove the burner phone, switching it on.

Light filters from my personal mobile, and Pete's name flashes on screen. I take a breath before taking Pete's call.

"Well?"

"She's just left your sister and brother-in-law." Pete's gruff voice fills the line.

"And?" Anger nips at the edges of my voice.

"She's leaving the hospital."

It is difficult to keep my voice even, and to not let my growing anger and alarm show. "Then stop her and bring her here." I terminate the call before Pete can respond.

The man is becoming a liability. Pete's ability to operate independently with any efficiency is dwindling away as I strengthen my hold on him. Pete does not function under pressure, and unfortunately this idiosyncrasy does not bode well for him.

Control slipping back into place, I turn the burner off, placing it back in the drawer. The office chair slides away from the desk and I walk over to the window, mentally preparing myself for the coming battle.

Kate has remembered something, I am positive. As I process this thought, I also admit amnesia had been a flimsy plan. If indeed her memory has returned – and I cannot be positive of this until Pete brings her back here – it would be inconvenient, but it isn't something I am not prepared for. When she's delivered, I can go back to Plan A.

This latest development can be used to my advantage, to pull her back in line. Her memory will assist me in getting what I want, and this time she will be fully aware of my intentions. So how do I ensure Kate/Chrissie's compliance? Easy. I threaten to take from her the things that she cares for the most.

Emotions are leverage. If you love someone or something, it can be used against you. I can bear witness to this, having viewed someone use my father's love for my mother against him. Illnesses are part of life. While medicines – like technology – move swiftly, they are not readily available to all. Mother's treatment nearly bankrupted us. Father may have celebrated the fact that she was well, as the medical world greedily counted the money rolling into their accounts, but this had a profound effect on me. My inheritance gone and forced to live below my status, I crawled from the gutter my father and mother sent us to, back into the world of the elite. It is why I never allow myself a personal life. It may appear, from the outside, that my life is empty. Yet, each time I take from someone what was taken from my father – from *me* – I have an overwhelming feeling of satisfaction. I have always had a strong tendency toward sociopathic behaviour. This detachment protects an emotional state of mind.

Walking back round my desk, I remove a plain brown envelope from the drawer. The photographs have been printed on A4 – I have a point to prove. Might as well make a statement of it. A smile tugs at my lips as the photographs fall onto the desk. Chrissie's husband, Simon, and their daughter Imogen's smiling faces stare back at me.

I'm bursting with pride, and I let the emotion shine within me, taking pleasure from the innocent faces. This will be all the encouragement Chrissie needs to leave her past behind, and embrace her sister Kate's life.

Chrissie will become as dead as my Kate. I will own her completely. She needs to know, to *understand*, that she is mine. If she doesn't, well, I haven't quite decided which one I will have killed first – her husband, Simon, or her lovely daughter, Imogen.

Pete isn't going to be happy about all this. Private investigators aren't cold-blooded killers. They never really like to dirty their hands. Pete has morals. They may be loose, but they are there, and manhandling women does not sit well within his moral spectrum.

But Pete doesn't have a choice. The way I see it, either he does what I tell him to do, or he ends up bleeding out in a Dumpster. Pete needs to understand that I am the puppet master. I pull his strings, and he dances to whatever tune I tell him to.

Jeff Green is my usual hitman. He is reliable and trustworthy. A professional. I have never met Jeff Green, which probably isn't his real name. The only contact I have for him sits in the burner. He knows how to charge. The money is wired to an overseas account.

I have already put out a hit on Pete. One phone call and Jeff will pull the trigger. Bye, bye, Pete. It will be a loss to my resources, but no one is irreplaceable.

Picking up the photographs off the desk, I place them back in the envelope just as the front door bangs open, signalling Kate and Pete's arrival.

Sitting down at my desk, I shuffle through some paperwork, preparing myself. Control washes over me as I wait for the office door to open.

I can hear Kate's voice through the wooden door. She doesn't sound happy. Unlike me, she isn't equipped for the battle ahead.

A knock sounds on the study door, and I take a second before answering, adding to the tension.

"Come in." I sit back in my chair, elbows resting on the arms of the Chesterfield, fingertips touching my lips.

Pete walks in, pulling Kate along at his side. His hand grips her arm.

Her eyes smoulder with anger as she pulls away from Pete's grip, tossing back her hair.

A distance of two feet separates them.

"Really, Liam, you didn't have to send the heavies in."

My Kate has gone, and Chrissie stands in front of me, her arms folded over her chest. A fire burns inside her, and I look forward to stamping it out.

"You didn't pick up any of my calls."

She rolls her eyes at me. With a sarcastic laugh, her hands fall to her hips. "And tell me, Liam. Out of curiosity, just who were you calling?"

While I have no fondness for Chrissie and the confident air that surrounds her, I will take immense pleasure in extinguishing it.

I remain sitting, my posture never changes, and the pleasure I am feeling remains hidden from sight. "You know who I was calling. I was calling you."

"Me? As in *Kate*?"

Part of me wonders what has triggered her memory. It is normal for human beings to feel curious. However, curious or not, it is of little consequence.

Chrissie is attractive when she is angry, I note.

"You see, that's the problem, Liam. I'm not Kate, and you bloody well know I'm not. Did you get your goon here to give me a good smack on the head? You must have been *sooo* happy when you found out I couldn't remember anything. After all, I'm betting that was the plan."

"Pete, leave us." My eyes never leave Chrissie's face.

"Don't bother, I'm going." She moves towards the door.

Pete hesitates and my anger erupts. "I said, *leave!*"

I look at Chrissie. This is the last time I will ever see her in my Kate. I point a finger at her. "You. You're staying right there."

"The hell I am. The thing is, Liam, you can't make me."

Ill-placed confidence rolls off her, and I smile, ready for the fun to begin.

"I wouldn't be so sure about that, Kate."

Her eyes sparkle with anger. *"I'm not Kate!"* Her hands clench at her sides, and her voice vibrates throughout the room.

Pete is stuck to the spot as though I have Super Glued him there.

"Get out!" I roar at him.

Squaring his shoulders, Pete leaves.

As the door closes, I turn to look at Chrissie. "You're not as bright as you think you are, Chrissie. Do you really think me stupid enough not have an insurance policy, something to keep you in check?"

Unease enters her eyes and I almost laugh out loud at her. Picking up the envelope, I throw it on the desk.

Chrissie eyes it with growing suspicion.

"Open it. I'm sure you will find the contents interesting."

She reaches for the envelope and the photographs fall onto the desk. Satisfaction crawls along my skin as she gasps and a series of emotions light her face – shock, fear, anger, resignation.

I smile.

Needing to assert my dominance further, I point at the photographs, my eyes never leaving her face. "Maybe you can help. You see, I can't decide which one I to have killed first. Such a difficult choice, wouldn't you say?"

Her eyes fly to mine, and in that moment, I see realisation dawn on her face. She is mine, and there is nothing she can do about it.

"You bastard." Her voice is nothing more than a whisper.

I smile at her, slow and sure.

Now all that is left for me to do is to get rid of Chrissie, and for my Kate to come back to me for good.

I am very much looking forward to breaking Chrissie's spirit and ripping her apart.

Chapter Fourteen

KATE

The photographs tumble from the envelope. My blood runs cold. Fear fills me, and I begin to shake. Simon and Imogen's images float before me. My eyes fly up, meeting Liam's. There is no part of me that doesn't believe him when he says he will have them killed. Nothing stands between Liam and what he wants. The amount of money he has helps bring his desires to fruition. Hate sears my skin like a hot knife.

Liam smiles. It is cruel, victorious, and egotistical. He knows he has won.

There is no point in standing here. I am only adding to Liam's pleasure. I pick up the photographs and turn to leave the room.

"I'm not finished."

Slowly, I turn to face him, watching as he walks around

the desk. Like a peacock fanning out its feathers, Liam's jaunt is one of self-assurance. I am a fly caught in a spider's web.

Does the real Kate – my sister – still exist, or has he killed her?

"What did you do with Kate?"

Revolution clouds his face. "She got cancer. No one leaves me, not until I say, and she got *cancer*."

Ahh… something Liam cannot control, and it eats away at him. Good.

I close my eyes against the pain. Part of me envies her. She is free of Liam, while I am stuck here. The other part of me grieves, knowing I have missed my opportunity to ever see my sister again. Pain stabs at my heart. Life with Liam is empty, and I hate the thought of Kate dying without any love or support from her family.

His fingers bite into my right arm. I know he has chosen this arm to cause me more pain. It is written in the cruel snarl on his lips. If he thinks I am going to cry out, he is wrong. I won't.

I pull my arm away from his wicked fingers.

His sharp blue eyes look like two pieces of cold hard stone, but I don't back down. He may have what he wants, but I will not cower in front of him.

"Drop it, Liam. You've won. I'm staying."

"It's not enough anymore."

Stunned, I stare at him. What more can he want or do to me?

He grabs the silk neckline of my dress and, in a swift yank, the fabric tears. The heels of my sandals clack against the wooden floor as I move away from him.

"Get off! I said, you've won, I'm staying. Leave me alone."

He smiles. "No."

Grabbing my arms, he shakes me until my teeth rattle and my vision blurs.

"I want my Kate back, and you are going to give her to me."

"I can't. I'm not Kate, and nothing you can do will change that, get off me!"

Fear makes my heart beat mad within my chest. My tongue darts out and I lick my dry lips. I look at the solid wooden door. Two metres stand between me and escape. Two metres have never seemed so far.

"You will be Kate."

Liam's hand whips through the air and strikes me across the face. I stumble and trip over the Persian rug. He's on me before I can get up, his fingers tearing at the fabric of my dress. My hands claw at his. He slaps me again before punching me in the stomach. His leg rests on my right thigh, pinning me down. Coughing, I try and take air into my lungs.

"You're wrong, you will be Kate. Once I've finished with you, there will *only* be Kate."

My heart skips a beat.

"I can't be Kate, I'm Chrissie!"

"No, you're Kate. You're *mine*."

I feel powerless and fragile. Breakable. I hate these emotions, hate them even more as Liam forces himself on me.

His hand slides between my legs and the thin lacy fabric of my knickers give. I scream at him to stop. My hands push at his body as my brain keeps telling me this can't be happening.

He removes his leg from mine, and I thrash beneath him.

"This is your problem. My Kate was always compliant."

"I'm not Kate!" I scream at him.

My throat is raw, my body hurts. I scream at him that I can never be anyone but me. I haven't seen Kate since I was a little girl. Back when my head was full of fanciful thoughts, of princesses and unicorns. How can I be Kate when I don't even know her?

"You are mine. The sooner you realize this, the easier it's going to be for you," Liam hisses at me.

"I'll *never* be yours." I shove at his shoulders as he pushes up my bra and squeezes my breasts hard between his fingers.

"I will *break* you."

With the skirt of my dress around my waist, I am conscious of how exposed and unprotected I am.

Liam pulls down his trousers and I scream as my brain acknowledges Liam's intention to rape me.

I scream and scream until my throat is sore, and the only noise I am capable of making is nothing more than a soft croak. My eyes close – not in surrender, no, never surrender. Seeing Liam's face above me as he rapes me is too much. There is no stopping him, I know that. It doesn't mean I have to watch him plough into me.

My body is sore and spent as I lie there.

Liam removes his body from mine and a gentle breeze falls across my exposed skin.

My eyes snap open to find him looking down at me.

He is euphoric in his victory, in raping me.

"Get out." He turns his back, dismissing me.

He doesn't have to tell me to leave twice. Gathering the photographs from the floor, I hold them against my chest and walk on shaky legs to the door. What is left of my knickers falls to the floor, and I leave them.

Liam might think he has won by raping me. That he has somehow broken me. But I won't let him. I am stronger than what he has done to me. And I will have my vengeance, though at the moment it is still unclear how I am going to achieve this.

He may abuse my physical body, but I will not let him have my mind as well. Having been robbed of my mind once, I am not going to let him take it again.

The door to his study remains open. He can close his own bloody door. The sound of my sandals against the marble filters across the hall. Taking them off, I throw them one at a time at a large Victorian Sèvres-style porcelain vase. The hand-painted vase crashes to the floor as my sandals hit it. Pieces of porcelain scatter around the feet of a late-nineteenth-century Black Forest bear side table. Out of all the antiques littering the house, I have always liked this table, with playful bears rolling around at each end while a larger bear laughs holding up the top.

Today, however, the table doesn't make me smile. No, the only satisfaction I feel is the look of anger on Liam's face as he emerges and surveys the damage.

"You stupid bitch!"

"I'm not Kate! I'm Chrissie!" I shout back at him before turning and slamming the bedroom door.

The lock slides into place with a click and I sink down onto the carpeted floor.

No, I'm not broken.

With shaking fingers, I remove the photographs from my chest, tears falling onto my husband Simon's image.

"I'm so sorry, baby."

I trace a finger over his face, wondering what he thinks has happened to me. The thought makes me cry and my sobs echo around me.

"I'm so sorry," I whisper over and over as I hold the

photographs to me.

On unsteady legs, I place the pictures in the drawer of the bedside table and strip off what is left of my clothes. The bathroom mirror shows Liam's abuse on my body. Desperate to get his scent off of me, I step into the shower and turn on the faucet. Cold water nips at my skin, and I scrub and scrub until my flesh turns red.

As I turn off the tap, I also turn off my feelings. Tears no longer pour from my eyes. I am still me, Chrissie Sanders.

Not Kate.

Chapter Fifteen

LIAM

A smile lights my face as I adjust the jacket of the three-piece Corneliani suit. Pulling on the sleeves of the white shirt, I expose a pair of turquoise Elsa Peretti cabochon cufflinks. Closing the door to Kate's bedroom I zip up my trousers.

It has taken three weeks, but today I feel progress is being made. Today, the fight was less physical. A few more days and Chrissie will be broken, and I will have my Kate back.

I never stop to think about the person I have become. There is freedom and enjoyment in being comfortable with one's actions and thoughts. Self-doubt is for the weak of mind. The Thorntons are old money, and as such there are certain expectations associated with someone of my class. There was the minor blip with Father's bad investment into Mother's health, but the status associated with old money always remains.

If I don't win by manipulation and business strategies, I win by other means. One way or another, I always get what I want. It is amazing how a simple car journey can be your last, or how easy it is to fall to your death. Jeff Green is inventive. Each death is linked to an unfortunate 'accident,' allowing control to slide back into my hands. Jeff is well worth his one-million-a-hit price tag.

Echoes of Kate moving around her room penetrate the wooden door. Maybe I will give things another week. My Kate never demonstrated such spirit and it is as frustrating as it is intoxicating. It has been a long time since anyone has defied me. Surprisingly, I find the challenge has stimulated my sexual interest in my wife. Another week should assist in satisfying my libido enough to curb such desires. I like to keep sex and personal relationships separate, preventing emotional entanglement.

Chrissie's defiance has heated my blood, and sex with her is more pleasurable than it ever was with my Kate. Still, pleasure is not designed to last forever, and I am aware that as I break Chrissie, the sexual gratification I receive will end.

The incident in my study has pushed back my meeting with Henry Henderson by a month. While I didn't feel I had hit Kate that hard, the bruising on her face says different. My business deal with Henry is a delicate affair, and the presence of his wife and child provides me with unseen leverage. With Kate unable to make an appearance, delaying our meeting had been my only option. Kate's presence is required to pander to Jane and their awful child.

Now that I know how easy Kate bruises, I ensure that any damage I inflict during our little sparring matches, our battle of wills, can be hidden with clothing. Adaptation is paramount when life is business. The world of the elite is built on appearances. They are illusions, but then so are such things as happiness and contentment.

"Hello!" Jenny's voice rings from the hall.

The wail of her baby follows her call. Why people feel the need to have them is beyond me. They are nothing more than a chain around your neck, tying you down and draining your finances.

"Anyone home?"

Irritation bites at my heels and my feet stop midway downstairs. What the hell is she doing here? Turning, I retrace my steps to Kate's room.

The room is empty and the sound of running of water draws me into the bathroom. As I open the door, Kate freezes mid step into the shower. Bruises litter her body, across the tops of her arms and upper thighs, along her breasts and stomach. The ones on her breasts are the worst.

Silently, I congratulate myself. Once dressed, even with three quarter sleeves, no one will see the injuries I have inflicted.

Suspicion shadows Kate's eyes.

"Jenny's here. Make sure you put on some makeup."

Like a beautiful ice sculpture, Kate remains frozen to the spot. I make a point of allowing my eyes to travel down her body.

"Put some trousers and a shirt on. I don't want you upsetting her." It is important that Kate feels my domination of her.

Her eyes blaze with anger. We both know she will comply to my demand.

Power, it is all about power.

My authority washes over her, hemming her in. Chrissie

may still be putting up a fight, but I am winning. She will become my Kate.

Turning, I close the door.

Jenny is halfway up the stairs as I step back onto the landing. Her floral Zimmermann maxi skirt trails on the steps. I note that her cami top makes her look frumpy, the shade too heavy for the light colours of the skirt. Jenny is still carrying a lot of post-baby weight. Her breasts are too large for the low-cut velvet top. Women with large breasts should learn to cover them up and wear something with more structure. It prevents them from looking cheap, as my sister does now. Jenny has never possessed any style, despite our money and status. If allowed, Jenny would be a hippy. I make a mental note to speak with her about her appearance. It is something that needs doing from time to time.

While I feel the need to tell her that with no makeup on, she looks homely, I don't. If I start listing her many flaws, I will be here all day.

Her dry curly hair falls past her jaw, and I wonder when she last visited the hairdresser. Jenny has let herself go, and motherhood does not suit her.

My crocodile Magnanni derby shoes beat hastily on the steps as I come to meet her. Taking hold of her arm, ensuring I keep a safe distance from the red-faced baby cradled against her chest, I steer her downstairs. The pink outfit the baby wears displays its gender. Babies are androgynous, which is why parents feel the need to clothe them in colours indicative of gender.

"You look well, Jenny." The insincerity of my compliment washes over her.

Jenny and Dennis have named the snivelling mass in the pink outfit Elsie after our deceased mother. Why she feels I need to be reminded of our mother by cooing her name at the baby in her arms is unfathomable.

Elsie. The name grates at me. It has been ten years since our parents died, rather suddenly, in a car accident along a country road. Jenny still mourns their loss. Our parents' deaths were the first time I used Jeff Green's services. Having experienced the benefits and liberation of ridding myself of them, it didn't take me long to realize Jeff Green's skills were useful in my business deals too.

The orchestrated deaths of my parents assisted in shaping me into the man I have become. I view it as one of my key triumphs. Father was beginning to get too interested in the way I conduct my business. Despite my subtle warnings, Father chose not to listen. His death was inevitable. Playing the part of the grieving son was draining at times, but no one could find fault with my performance. Their funeral was a lavish affair, as expected for someone of their breeding. While they lowered the coffins into the ground, I congratulated myself on a job well done.

The death of my parents provided freedom, and I embraced it. Whitegates, the billions worth of investments, and the lives I control. I owe it all to a sound business arrangement between me and Jeff Green, and the death of my parents.

Jenny isn't capable of understanding. She is too much like Mother. Too sweet and nice, always thinking of others and trying to please.

"Why don't you settle yourself in the orangery? I'll get Mrs. Jones to bring in some refreshments. Kate won't be long."

The baby lets out a wail.

"I have some business that needs attending to."

"Can't you stay for a bit? It seems like ages since we have

spent time together."

"I'm sorry, Jenny. I can't, not today. You should have rung and let me know you were coming."

Tears swim in her eyes and I wish she would use her time more effectively, for instance by shutting up the thing in her arms.

Walking over to her, I place a light kiss on her forehead. "Perhaps another time. Now, let me see if I can find Mrs. Jones."

Mrs. Jones is a stocky woman with dyed dark-brown hair that doesn't suit her pale complexion or age. She is no beauty. Her features are too sharp and her jaw too masculine. Her hair started turning grey in her early twenties. Now in her mid-fifties, she has developed the unfortunate habit of dyeing it back to its original colour. White roots spring up along her parting, making her look older.

Mrs. Jones is also a heavy smoker, and the effects of her nicotine addiction can be seen in the lines ravaging her face. I do not allow her to smoke while at Whitegates. The white walls remain tarnish free, and the garden and bins remain free of cigarette ends. The scent of her addiction follows her and lingers in the air around her.

While her smoking is irksome, I overlook it. Mrs. Jones is excellent at her job – organising the cleaning staff and ensuring that refreshments are at hand for unexpected guests. She also knows when to be seen, and when to remain hidden from view.

Apart from Jake, and now Jake Junior, Mrs. Jones is the only regular employee at Whitegates. The cleaning staff are from an agency and come once a week. I like my privacy. I also don't feel the need to prove myself by employing people to open my front door.

With the exception of Jenny, Jake is the only person who ties me to my past. As a boy, I spent hours amongst the roses, listening to his stories. My favourite of Jake's tales from his younger years is the one about the Russians who burnt the neighbours' house down. Jake, as he tells the story, was woken by the smell of smoke, and having rung the fire brigade, he broke in and rescued a sleeping boy and his family next door. It is quite a tale.

Jake is my only indulgence. There is no logic to this indulgence. I only know that, for some unexplainable reason, I cannot and will not let Jake go. The thought of losing him is inconceivable. It is a weakness I seem unable to relinquish, and so I choose to ignore it. This is why I employ Jake Junior.

The soft tread of footsteps sounds on the marble floor and I stop as I approach the study to watch Kate descend the stairs. She is a rare beauty, with her silken long black hair and soft almond-shaped emerald eyes. Her caramel skin glistens against the fabric of the asymmetric-printed Tommy Hilfiger foulard shirt. The fluidity of the shirt wafts around her as she walks. Tailored red Claudie Pierlot trousers emphasise the long, lean sculpture of her legs. Ivory Paciotti mules with red Swarovski-crystal chain trims bring the outfit to a sumptuous end.

I take pleasure not only in how exquisite Kate looks, but also in her compliance to my command to wear a shirt and trousers.

The gurgling noise of Jenny's baby drifts through the hall, and Kate's lips curve upwards in response. Transfixed, I watch her make her way towards the orangery.

She is a luscious vision, and she is all mine.

Chapter Sixteen

KATE

The bathroom door opens and Liam walks in. A look of irritation lines his face. I am positive I can't be the source of his irritation. Not even Liam has enough energy for a second round of this morning's activities. We are both spent, in more ways than one. And only one of us is taking any pleasure from our union. It's not me.

My left hand balls at my side, hidden from his sharp blue eyes as he stands there taking in the bruises he has caused.

My emotions are all over the place, and I pray that none of them are showing on my face.

Liam has raped me every day since the incident in the library. Other than changing the area of my body he hits, not much has altered. The reason for the modification is simple – a trophy wife cannot be shown off to its optimum if it appears damaged.

I view my better understanding of Liam as research, because at some point I will have gathered enough information on him to formulate a plan for freedom.

As Liam's eyes wander over my body, I refuse to move or look away. There is no way I will let him break me. I am not about to give him that kind of power over me. *I will not be broken. I'm Chrissie. I will not become Kate.* The words have become a silent mantra in my head. Each time Liam abuses me, they rattle around, and I remind myself it is only my body he's taking, nothing more.

"Jenny's here. Make sure you put on some makeup."

I want to punch him.

"Put some trousers and a shirt on. I don't want you upsetting her." Having made his point, Liam turns, closing the door behind him.

If he thinks I missed the slight smile that touched his lips, he's wrong. I will wear the shirt and trousers and let him think he is exercising his control over me. But I will not become his victim.

My legs do not agree, and they shake, along with my hands, as I walk into the shower.

I will not be broken. I'm Chrissie. I will not become Kate.

The water stings as it hits my skin. I scrub Liam from my body, wishing I could so easily scrub him from existence.

Hair shampooed and conditioned, I turn off the water and pat my skin dry. I smooth arnica gel over the bruises. The tropical anti-inflammatory treatment works to reduce the bruising from Liam's attacks, and eases the ache in my screaming muscles.

The cool silk of a lace-trim Carine Gilson kimono robe folds round my body as I tie the belt. While I have no fondness for designer clothing, more because it represents Liam than anything else, the robe has a sumptuous feel to it. While I appreciate the soft golden fabric against my tender skin, getting rid of Liam would achieved this in a permanent and more pleasant way. I pull a silk shirt off the hanger and grab a pair of red trousers and ivory mules. The colours provide a contrast and the outfit does not press against my bruised skin. Unlike the lace bra I'm wearing beneath it.

Anger fills me as the bra digs into the bruises, and I lift the shirt to move the bra hook onto the last eyelet to lessen some of the pressure. A tear falls down my cheek and I swipe it away, unaware I am crying until it rolled down my face. The tear sits on my fingers, and others fall to join it. Hands clenching, I will myself not to cry. To cry is to let Liam win, and I will not allow him the satisfaction.

Oxygen fills my lungs as I inhale deep. Sitting on the padded bench in the wardrobe, I concentrate on my breath as it enters and leaves my body. A tune replaces my sadness and anger. Over and over it plays, and I tell myself, *If I don't think, then I won't feel, and if I don't feel, I will survive this.*

Staring down at the missing lock on the bedroom door, I give myself a mental telling off. *Don't think, don't feel, survive.*

I close the bedroom door and step onto the landing. My heels sing out a beat, merging with the tune in my head. It is Imogen's favourite nursery rhyme, 'The Grand Old Duke of York'. She likes it because it has York in the title, and we live in York.

The soft gurgle of Elsie's voice drifts over to me as I reach the hall, and my lips curl into a smile at the sound. Thoughts of innocence, happiness, and contentment wash over me. In my world of coldness and brutality, it is a welcome noise.

Following the sound of Elsie's burbling, I walk towards the orangery.

Mrs. Jones sets down a tray filled with coffee, tea, and biscuits. Her black dress makes her shoulders appear extra wide, like she has forgotten to remove the clothes hanger. Thick legs poke out from beneath the respectable knee-length hemline. Her hair is ready for dyeing again, judging by the length of the white roots on display. I don't understand her obsession with using such a dark colour when her hair is obviously white. There are plenty of stunning women and men with grey hair.

My nose wrinkles at the smell of stale tobacco coming off her, and I try to iron out my features as she turns. A look of disapproval shines in her eyes, and I wonder what I have done, either as my sister or myself, to make her dislike me so much.

Arms outstretched, I ignore Mrs. Jones as she leaves the room. "Come on, Elsie, let your favourite auntie have a hug."

Jenny beams and Elsie gurgles as I take her into my arms. I coo at her.

"You're a natural mum," I tell Jenny. "I don't know why you worry so much." I'm referring to the number of messages I receive from her a day. "You know all new mums worry, it's a very natural thing. You're doing a great job, Jenny." I sit down next to her as Elsie blows a bubble at me.

"Do you think you and Liam will ever have kids?"

I blink at Jenny, stunned by the question.

It is natural, given the circumstances, that Jenny would ask, but inside I quiver at the thought of a little Liam running around the place. It is not something I want to contemplate. Shivers ripple down my spine.

"I don't think Liam's work allows him space for children." I congratulate myself on my diplomacy.

Jenny frowns. "It just seems wrong. You're so good with

Elsie. You'd make a great mum."

I feel the burning need to tell Jenny I already *am* a mum, that I have a beautiful daughter. And that, prior to Liam, my husband Simon and I had talked about having another baby. Liam not only stripped everything I love away from me, he also destroyed my future. Mine and Simon's.

Imogen's face shimmers in front of me, and I wonder if she knows how much her mummy loves her. Tears swim in my eyes and I look down at Elsie so Jenny can't see them, blinking them away. Elsie blows me another bubble, and a smile falls over my lips as I breathe in the smell of baby powder.

Jenny's hand touches my knee. "I'm sorry, Kate, I didn't mean to pry. Sometimes I think Liam doesn't have his priorities in order."

Poor Jenny. If only she knew the truth.

Emotions under control, I paste my best smile on my lips. "Now, that's enough of that. You didn't come here to talk about me and Liam. You came to show off this wonderful little girl of yours. And so you should. She's beautiful, just like her mum."

"She is beautiful, isn't she? It's strange, but I don't think I knew what love really was until Elsie screamed her way into the world. Not that I don't love Dennis, of course I do, it's just that this love I feel for Elsie... Why, I would do anything within my power to ensure her happiness. It's almost scary."

I jiggle Elsie in my arms, freeing a hand and laying it on top of hers. "Welcome to motherhood. Children are special. It's why we love them so much."

Elsie's face scrunches up. Her mouth opens and she fills the orangery with her indignant cries.

"I think she's getting hungry."

"I only a couple of hours ago."

"I don't think Elsie can tell the time yet, and right now she wants feeding."

Elsie puckers up her lips and graces us with her best 'feed me' cry.

Jenny laughs as she holds her daughter. "She's just like her mum. I'm always hungry too."

"In that case, I'd better start pouring you a cup of tea. And I think if we leave those biscuits any longer, they'll go soft and won't be worth eating."

"You're the best, Kate."

Elsie latches onto Jenny's breast and contented little sucking noises echo through the room.

Chapter Seventeen

JESSICA

Staring into the toilet, my legs resting on the cold tile floor, I wait for the sickness to pass. Three weeks of morning sickness and I am already fed up with sitting here feeling lousy. Why they call it morning sickness baffles me because I am fine in the morning. The *afternoon* is when the sickness hits.

I lower myself onto the floor, enjoying the feeling of the cool ceramic as I gather the energy to stand up and brush my teeth. In every situation there is a winner, and my dentist will be ecstatic about how many times I now brush my teeth in a day.

OK, I tell myself, *I can do this.* I push myself off the floor, smoothing down the front of my summer dress. The bright-yellow fabric is a good deal sunnier than I feel. A soft click flows from the front door, and footsteps sound on the stairs.

At the moment, Charles won't have to look too far to find me.

Taken by another wave of sickness, I sink back down onto the cold floor. It appears I'm not finished yet.

Blue denim appears next to me and warm hands pull the hair from my face as I grip the toilet. Not the most romantic image I've ever pictured for us, but I am grateful Charles is here. A glass of cold water dangles in front of me and I take it, spitting the contents into the toilet. We sit in silence for a few minutes, each of us trying to gauge if the sickness is over for another day.

"Do you feel like you can move yet?"

My head tilts and I begin assessing how I feel. This time the nausea has passed, and I can feel the slightest relief. A toothbrush makes its way to me, and once again I give my teeth a brush. As soon as I finish, Charles takes the toothbrush and scoops me up. My head falls onto his chest and I rub my cheek against the soft fabric of his t-shirt.

Together, we tumble onto the sofa, my bottom sinking into the feather cushions, my legs draped over his knees. The sofa is too big for the room, but it enables us both to stretch out in the evening, so I don't care.

Charles hands me a pack of dry crackers.

I lean into the crook of his arm. The crackers help settle my stomach. Time passes and I enjoy just being with this incredible man. At moments like this, I have to keep telling myself this isn't a dream, but reality.

Charles' right hand rests on my stomach. The gesture makes me smile, and I feel like a cat all snug on a cold rainy day. My bump is a gentle swell at the moment, but I love every tiny inch of it.

In a few days, I will reach my third trimester, a huge milestone for me and our baby. Every day, I stand in front of the mirror looking at my expanding stomach, and it hits me – I am happy and loved. It's like a bomb going off inside me, touching every module and atom. Contentment spreads through every part of me, and I never stop feeling grateful.

"I think I'll have to get some new clothes soon. Things are starting to get a little tight." I use the pack of crackers to point at my belly.

"Why don't we go shopping on Saturday?"

"Sounds good. We'll need to get an early start. I don't fancy throwing up in the public toilets."

Charles chuckles. "Oh, I think I can manage to *rise* early." Wickedness dances in his eyes.

I laugh, playfully swiping him on the chest. "That's what got me in this position in the first place!"

"There's nothing wrong with the position you're in. In fact, I can definitely see a lot of benefits to it."

Charles' hand moves over my stomach, tracing the tops of my thighs and sneaking under the skirt of my cotton dress. My breath catches in my throat as his hand runs tantalisingly up my leg. The crackers fall to the floor as I reach for Charles. Turning, I pick them up, so I don't stand on them later, setting them down on the coffee table. The headline on the newspaper catches my eye. *'Tycoon Files for Bankruptcy.'*

"What?" I grab the paper, looking at the photo of Henry Henderson.

Profits slumped for Henderson Corp when a vicious takeover by Sitcom Industries caused stocks to plummet. Self-made tycoon Henry Henderson was left destitute. His wife left him following the death of their son, Jamie, from a congenital heart defect, only days after he filed for bankruptcy…

My hands tremble and I am transported back into Liam's world. I will never understand why Liam feels the need to play with and destroy so many lives. I have always liked Henry Henderson. He is… *was*… a big jolly teddy bear.

"What's wrong?" Charles takes the crumpled newspaper from my hands, looking at the article. His face pale as he reads.

"Sitcom Industries is one of Liam's offshore businesses. I wonder if Henry was aware of that?" I pause as I consider my question. "No, I doubt it. Liam's relationship with the company is buried pretty deep." I look at Charles. "Why does he have to do it? It's not like Henry was hurting anyone. I just don't understand."

"I don't know. Liam has changed so much since we were boys. I don't even recognise him anymore."

Charles folds the paper, placing it back on the coffee table. He pulls my legs with him as he leans against the back of the sofa. "He can't hurt you anymore, Jess."

I trail my fingers along his jaw. "I know, baby. It just makes me sad when I see the destruction Liam is capable of. And for what? Because Liam doesn't like self-made money?"

"I don't know."

"Neither do I." Sadness taints my voice.

"Come on, you haven't got time to be sad." Charles swings my legs off the sofa, reaching for my cream cardigan. "Let's go for a walk on the beach and let the wind take it away."

Hands on my hips, I try to look stern. "I'll only go if you promise not to throw me in the sea."

"I didn't throw you in the sea! As I remember, I was piggybacking you and you *followed* me into the sea."

My finger rests against his chest. "You, mister, are not that innocent."

Wide hazel eyes full of fake virtue stare back at me.

"*Moi?*"

"Yes, you."

Innocence gives way to mischievousness. "Hey, if you want wicked, you only have to ask."

I yelp as Charles swings me up and carries me through to the kitchen. Scooping up the picnic blanket as he passes, he walks out the back door.

"You know, there are advantages to living so close to a quite-unpopulated beach. And I intend to explore every one of them." His deep voice rumbles with intention.

The grass tickles my feet as Charles lowers me to the ground.

"Oh, you do, do you? Well, in that case, I'll race you. Whoever wins gets to explore their creative talents on the other first."

I leap into a run, my strides long. I giggle as Charles swears at my swiftness. He comes charging at me like a bull and I speed up, knowing he has already lost.

Running is my thing. It got me through many difficult times while living with Liam. When I run, I don't think, I just listen to the pounding of my feet and the music blaring in my ears. Now, though, I am doing an awful lot of thinking, and most of it is directed at Charles and what I intend to do to his body.

The thought gets my feet moving faster. My breath catches in my throat, there's a smile on my lips, and the bull charging my way is left eating the sand I kick up.

Chapter Eighteen

LIAM

The newspaper sits on the edge of my desk. Satisfaction has my lips curling as I read the headline *'Tycoon Files for Bankruptcy'*. Picking up the paper, I sit back, relaxing into the ox-blood leather chair. With the exception of rescheduling my meeting with Henry Henderson due to Kate's injuries, everything has gone according to plan.

Looking over at the Queen Anne chairs by the Rembrandt, I allow my memory of that meeting to replay before me.

The Hendersons arrive on time, as is expected. Kate takes Jane and the brat outside as I show Henry into the study. Despite the brightness of the day, the sun doesn't penetrate far into the room. Guiding Henry over to the leather chairs at the rear of the room, I ignore the contract sitting on my desk, not wanting to appear overeager.

Henry sits, taking the whisky I offer him. He swirls it round the crystal tumbler, watching the ice clink. Silence fills the room and I allow it to cast its weight over us as I sip at the sweet, rich Glenmorangie 1975 Tain L'Hermitage. The peppery dried grass and malt finish sits on my tongue long after the intense top notes of cloves, aniseed, and stewed fruit have left.

Henry's blue check Canali suit adds to his expanding waistline. Checks are always a bad option when you are carrying excess weight. His open-collared white shirt (no tie) adds to the disorder. It is extraordinary how a person can make expensive clothing look cheap. While instinct has my toes curling with distain, I do not let it show on my face, though my fingers cannot help smoothing down my single-breasted black Brioni suit. The stylish, sophisticated Italian design flatters my trim frame. A silk Burberry tie nips at my neck in a Windsor knot, keeping my appearance professional and business-like. Henry's lack of tie highlights his lack of class. However irritating his dress and presence are, I take pleasure in knowing that, after today, Henry will be falling back into the gutter where he belongs, taking his wife and brat with him.

A number of bad investments have led Henry to this point. Of course, Henry is unaware of my involvement, or how much money I have made in the process. As one company falls, another waits to grab it. Sitcom Industries is a predatory company, snapping up and tearing businesses apart. It has a bad reputation, though the stock market favours it and shares remain buoyant. It is amazing how easy business dealings can be sometimes.

Henry doesn't have an appreciation of money and the power it holds, nor does he conduct himself with or understand the chicanery certain business dealings require. That is the problem with self-made money.

Despite Henry's background, he is considered a decent and honest man. Business does not value such traits, and predators take advantage.

Business makes an allowance for lack of veracity, and it supports subtlety.

Jane's shrill voice filters into the study from the hall through a slight gap in the study door. I have purposely left it ajar. Jane is loud and that awful child of theirs even louder. It provides an adroit reminder that this deal is Henry's only route if he wants to keep his company afloat, though he will no longer be the major shareholder. I smile inwardly at my own shrewdness, aware that, as this business proposal plays out, both Henry and I will seem to lose a vast amount of money. This is true for Henry. However, as the owner of Sitcom Industries, I stand to make a killing. What is that old-fashioned phrase people favour? Ah, yes, 'What one hand giveth, the other taketh away'. Within a month of signing the contract, Henry will be back in the gutter where he belongs, with the riffraff and trash. Also known as the middle class.

Even their title 'middle class' shows they can never achieve anything real. And, well, even if they do, like Henry has done, there is always someone like me waiting, ready to take it from them, sending them back down to where they belong.

Henry smiles at the sound of Jane's voice.

The door crashes open and Jamie runs in.

"Daddy, Daddy, can we go now? I want to ride Butch." Butch is a shabby brown Shetland pony that is anything but butch.

"Pleeeease, Daddy."

And here comes the pressure for Henry to sign the contract.

Adoration falls across Henry's face as his son pleads with him. "Now, Jamie, you know Daddy has some business to do. Why don't you go out in the garden with Mummy and Kate?"

Jamie's lips pucker. "They're being boring and talking nonsense."

Henry chuckles, his stomach wobbling. "That's women for you, son."

I lean forward, resting my whisky glass on the chair arm. "Why don't you ask Kate to take you to see Jake?"

The kid pouts and I force a smile to my lips. "Jake has had lots of adventures. Why don't you ask him about when the Russians burned down his neighbours' house?"

Jamie's face scrunches up in thought. "Were they real Russians?"

"As real as you and me," I encourage him.

As a man entering his late thirties, I now see Jake's Russian adventure for what it is — a work of fiction. Still, it is a story that a small boy will enjoy.

Jamie turns on his heel and runs to the door. "Kate! Kate! Kate!"

Henry chuckles as his son jumps from foot to foot while waiting for Kate to make her appearance.

Seconds can seem like hours, and I can feel damage being inflicted on my eardrums.

By the time Kate makes an appearance, my grip on my whisky glass has turned my knuckles white.

I send her a cool look as she enters the study.

Henry's eyes travel down Kate's slender body, lingering on her long, lean legs.

Dolce & Gabbana tropical rose-print shorts brush her high thighs. She wears a white Alexandre Vauthier blouse, tied at her waist, the bell sleeves ballooning around her thin arms. Her hair sits in a high ponytail, swishing down her back like a rope ready to be pulled. My fingers itch to grab at it, to force her head back and capture her mouth. Force my will on her and claim her.

She catches me looking at her and quickly walks over, taking Jamie's hand in hers. A smile graces her lips as she looks at the child, now dancing around the room singing, "Russians, Russians."

"Jake is going to tell Jamie about his Russian adventure."

Kate nods and leads the brat out the door.

Sipping my whisky, I sit back in my chair, enjoying the quiet.

Henry shuffles, draining his glass. There is no avoiding the elephant in the room any longer. It is time for him to sign the contract.

"Shall we?" I tilt my head towards the desk.

"Of course."

Henry wipes his hands down the length of his trouser legs. A slight sheen of sweat dampens his forehead.

So as not to overwhelm Henry, and to reinforce my nonchalant appearance, I remain where I am. My signature already graces the paper. Now all that is required is for Henry to add his.

I watch him read the contract. His legal team have already received a copy and have approved it. There is nothing within the contract to indicate the final outcome.

Picking up the Caran d'Ache Caelograph Zenith I have left next to the contract, Henry adds his signature.

"A refill?" I ask.

"Why not?" Henry raises his glass. "To new beginnings."

"Indeed, to new beginnings."

And bankruptcy.

Chapter Nineteen

KATE

Sweat trickles down my back, my breath an even rhythm as I approach the steps leading to the patio. A yoga mat sits on the concrete in readiness for my stretches. The air smells of fresh cut grass.

Kicking off my trainers, I stop the app – noting the distance, time, and stride – and change the music to a more tranquil beat. Yoga helps not only with strength and stretching out my muscles, but it creates balance and internal awareness of body and mind.

The sun kisses my face as I sit cross-legged on the mat in Sukhasana, my heart returning to its natural rhythm I begin meditating. Conscious thought fades. I become aware only of my breath as I inhale and exhale. Any thoughts of Liam fall away as I centre on healing my mind in readiness for our next battle.

Opening my eyes, they focus on Jake as he removes the deadheads from the flowers. He waves and wanders over. Arthritis eats at his joints, causing him to limp. Jake is a proud man, so I don't offer him any assistance up the steps. Instead, I move, coming to sit on the middle step so he doesn't have to climb them all.

"Morning, Jake." I send him a smile as he lowers his body onto the step next to me.

A sigh escapes his lips as he looks across the garden. "There's something that's been puzzling me for a while. I've not said anything, because, I guess, I've needed to do some thinking before I did."

Jake turns to face me. "You're not Kate."

Stunned, I say nothing, though my heart is beating so fast I can feel it in my throat.

"You see, I'm wondering why you've taken her place."

Jake's old face scrunches in thought as he waits for my response. Fear coats my skin in a thin layer of sweat as Simon and Imogen's faces shimmer before me. There's no point in lying, but what about my husband and daughter? Would I be putting them in danger if I told Jake the truth? No one controls Jake, not even Liam, so I don't have to worry about this being some kind of perverted test – even if the thought floats through my head.

If I can't lie, then only the truth remains. Fatigue crawls through my veins.

"No, my name is Chrissie. I'm Kate's twin sister."

"Yep, thought was the case."

My throat tightens as I think about my sister. "Liam said Kate got cancer."

Jakes nods. "Aye, I dare say that's what Liam believes."

The rustling of fabric and the clicking of old joints sound

as Jake stretches out his left leg. A groan escapes his lips as the worn green cords pull at the knees. Reaching into the back pocket of his trousers, he removes a small piece of paper. His eyes linger on it.

"Kate never had cancer."

I look up at him, hope shining in my eyes. If she never had cancer, she's still alive, which means she found a way out of Liam's control. Inside, I smirk. *Back at you, Liam.* I feel no resentment towards Kate for my present predicament, just relief. No one could have foreseen Liam's next move when his real wife supposedly died.

Kate is still alive, and that means I still have a chance of finding her one day. At the moment, with Liam around, finding Kate isn't an option. But Liam will get old and die. Then I will be free to find her. Ten years or twenty, it doesn't matter to me. All that matters is that Kate is still alive, and I still have a chance of finding her – one day.

Perhaps, maybe, like with Kate, there will be a chance to see Imogen again, to be with her and let her know Mummy loves her. I have to accept that Simon will move on and find someone else. It would be selfish of me to expect him not to. Expect him to stagnate. Time, no matter what they tell you, doesn't heal. There will always be a place in my heart where Simon lives.

"Kate's living with that doctor of hers."

Jake's voice rouses me from my thoughts.

"She thought no one knew, but Kate couldn't hide the truth from me. I'd seen the way they looked at each other." A smile touches his lips. "She deserves to be happy. I told her that when she left. I knew she'd find a way to make things work."

Tears swim in Jake's eyes, confusion clear on his face.

"Why'd you take her place? Kate went to such lengths to keep you a secret."

My eyes rest on my hands, hiding my pain. "I'm not here by choice, believe me. I don't even know how Liam found out about me. Though I think it has something to do with that thug of his, Pete Townsend. I think he's the reason I ended up in the hospital with amnesia.

"Replacing me with my sister was easy. Who would suspect a thing? We look the same, and my memory loss helped with any differences in our personalities. God, I can't believe how lucky he was. I mean, what are the chances of hitting my head just right and giving me amnesia?" Bitterness clings to my words. I'm through pretending, and Jake has provided me with the chance to vent my frustrations. With no lies or secrecy.

"I hate him, Jake. I never thought I could hate someone the way I hate Liam. There's nothing I can do. I'm stuck here." My hands ball in my lap.

"He knows about my daughter and husband. He said that he would have them killed if I didn't become Kate."

Jake's hand rests on my shoulder, gently pulling me to him. As my tears fall, I bury my head in the crook of his neck.

"Shh, shh, lass. There's a solution to most things. We just have to find one."

Jake's earthy smell fills my senses as my sobs lessen, turning into small hiccups.

"I don't know how to stop him, Jake. Look at what Liam did to Henry Henderson. He ripped that poor man's life apart, and Henry doesn't even know that it was Liam who did it. *I* know, though. I don't know how Liam did it, but he did. Henry has lost everything – his kid, his wife, his home. I can't afford for that to happen to those I love."

"Come on, lass, let's not give up."

I take the hanky he offers, blowing my nose and wiping at my tears.

Head resting on his shoulder, I look across at the flowers, staring at them without seeing them.

"How did you know?"

Jake smiles, handing me the piece of paper in his hand.

My fingers shake as I unfolded it. Staring at a photograph of Kate and me when we were kids, I feel fresh tears form. Our little arms are thrown around each other, our heads touching as we smile at the camera. The photograph was taken when we were around five. Before our parents died.

"She asked me to keep this safe for her. I think she was afraid that Liam would find it."

My fingers trace over the photograph, following the lines of our identical pink dresses. Even for me, it was difficult to tell us apart. Only our eyes are distinct. Kate's are softer, full of hope and dreams, whereas mine hold the hard edge of stubbornness. Kate was always the more submissive of us, going out of her way to make everyone happy.

"No two people are alike. From a glance, it's easy to be deceived. People don't recognise the subtle differences. They're unable to see through the outside of a person to where the main differences lie. I can." Jake takes a breath. "You may *look* like Kate, but I see that you're not."

With a pang of sorrow, I hand him the photograph and watch him fold it, placing it back in its hiding place.

Jake gives the pocket a reassuring pat. "Your secret's safe. I'm not a blabber."

"Thank you."

Jake Junior strides around the side of the house, a spade balancing on his shoulder. There's a jaunt to his steps and he's singing Johnny Paycheck's 'Take This Job and Shove It'. He might be out of tune, but his song choice makes me laugh. I wipe the last of the tears from my eyes as Junior takes the spade and strums it like a guitar.

Jake's white eyebrows lift as he watches Junior strut across the lawn towards the flowerbeds. "I don't know what he thinks he's digging up, but whatever it is, I'd better go save it."

As I sit and watch the two men talk, a wave of sickness grips me and I clutch my stomach. Grabbing my trainers, I run the last few yards into the house, to the downstairs cloakroom.

Most people's cloakrooms are small, containing the necessary toilet and sink. Not Liam's. In addition to the toilet and sink is a large ornate nineteenth-century French marble-top gilt table. It has to be the ugliest table I have ever seen. A large gilt mirror from the same century matches the table not only in style but ugliness. Against the back wall is a Michael Fairclough painting, the title of which is *At Sea - Dog Watch VI*. There's no dog, and other than a bit of yellow and orange, there isn't much to watch. It is fair to say I am not a lover of Michael Fairclough, but then I don't have much appreciation for fine art.

I would also be so bold as to say that Liam doesn't like Michael Fairclough either, given the painting's position in the house.

"Kate!" The devil (Liam) shouts.

Ignoring him, I sink to the floor, raise the toilet lid, and begin emptying the contents of my stomach. Sweat prickles along my skin, and my hands shake as I place them on the cold tile floor and sink my body down. I find the cool surface soothing as I bring my knees to my chest.

"Kate!" He sounds annoyed.

Liam's footsteps drum against the floor, the sound bringing him closer and closer to me. I look at the door, acknowledging too late that I should have closed it. His black shoes appear in the doorway as another wave of sickness washes over me.

Shoes tapping, he waits for me to finish, a look of disgust falling over his features.

I haven't felt this bad so suddenly since I was pregnant with Imogen, and the thought strikes a chord of recognition in my head. I feel the overwhelming need to cry. *Oh, God, no! I can't be!*

Stomach heaving, I throw up, confirming what I already know. I'm pregnant. My periods have never been regular and, with the amnesia and the constant battles with Liam, missing it went unnoticed. Now, as I gaze into the toilet, all I can think is how much I *don't* want to be pregnant, with Liam's child.

He's still tapping his shoe against the tiles. The tapping has become more persistent as his irritation rises.

Inside, I snigger. If my being sick is an inconvenience, wait until he finds out I am pregnant. 'Ecstatic' is not a word I'd link to my *own* feelings on the matter. Liam, I am sure, is going to be even less so.

"Kate!"

I look up at him from the toilet, tears rolling down my face from too much vomiting and the miserable knowledge of the life that grows inside me.

"The marquee people are here. I need you to organise them."

Disbelief makes my eyes as large and round as saucers.

With a lot of effort, I peel myself away from the toilet and sag against the wall. "Sorry, Liam, I'm a bit busy at the moment." I point at the toilet.

"Well, I can't do it. I have more important things to do."

"Seriously, Liam, it's not going to happen. Get Mrs. Jones to sort them out." As if on cue, my body heaves and I slump back over the toilet.

"What's wrong with you?"

The lack of care or warmth in his voice chills me.

"Oh, I'll tell you what's wrong, Liam. I'm pregnant, that's what's wrong here."

Horror replaces his irritation.

"I bet you never took that into account while you were raping me."

"I did not rape you. You're my wife."

As I am in no position to thump him, I resort to lifting my eyebrows at him. "No, Liam, we both know that technically isn't correct. I'm actually your sister-in-law. You know, the one you and your thug knocked down some stairs? And, by the way, even if I *was* your wife, no still means no, and rape is still rape."

He surges forward, his hands balling at his sides.

My body convulses and he takes a step back as I throw up.

"You're going to have to get rid of it."

I lay my hand on my stomach. *'Get rid of it.'* I couldn't. The thought fills me with dread.

Moving away from the toilet, I look at him as he stands there in his dark-grey Stefano Ricci suit and Magnanni Oxford brogues. He cuts a nice picture – if you don't mind the ice in his blue eyes.

"I'm not about to kill an innocent baby, even if that child is yours."

It isn't the baby's fault that its father is a cold, unfeeling bastard. Life is life to me. There's no way I can get rid of it, even if the child is Liam's.

"You will get rid of it, *Kate.*"

His voice slices through me like ice.

I make the decision not to reply and throw up in the toilet instead. When I come back up, Liam is gone, and I slump down onto the cold tiles in relief.

Today is Liam's turn to hold a charity event, hence the marquee. The thought does not fill me with excitement. While I am no longer required to oversee the installation of the marquee, I will be required to makes an appearance, as hostess.

Running a hand over my face as I lie on the tiles, I wonder how I am going to prevent Liam from killing my baby.

Chapter Twenty

LIAM

The first of our guests are arriving and Kate still hasn't made an appearance. Anger festers in the pit of my stomach, despite the smile I place on my lips. Unable to leave my post by the stairs, I prepare to meet our guests.

This is not the Hendersons'. I am more than aware of the protocol my class demands. The toe of one crocodile Stemar Oxford shoe beats against the marble floor. I run a hand along the satin-trim Tom Ford Shelton tuxedo, adjusting the velvet bowtie at my neck.

Paula Clarkson sashays through the open front doors, fuchsia-pink lips set in a thin line. A pink, Maticevski, one-shoulder gown hugs her curves. Her arm is linked through John Templeton's in a casual yet dominant manner. It would appear that someone had a disagreement on the journey here.

Paula has had so much Botox injected into her face, it is

now her mannerisms that give her feelings away, rather than the usual facial expressions.

I step forward. "Why, Paula, you look lovely tonight." Leaning in, I air-kiss both cheeks.

"John." I take the man's hand in mine.

It is a weak handshake. His fingers hardly fold around my hand.

John's jaw drops and Paula's back stiffens, her eyes narrowing in jealousy.

I turn to see Kate gliding downstairs. She is a true vision of beauty in a fitted white Roland Mouret Galloway strapless gown. The fabric elegantly falls onto the Jimmy Choo Sacora 100 satin pearl sandals. Her black hair is artfully piled on top of her head, strands falling in soft curls around her face, tickling the three-row cultured-pearl choker around her neck. A smile plays on her glossy rose-tinted lips. Her emerald eyes sparkle in warning.

I shift in apprehension. Chrissie is back.

"Paula, John, I must apologise for my tardiness." Kate leans forward, air-kissing Paula's rigid face.

John, on the other hand, is more than eager for any excuse to get closer to Kate.

Formalities over, Kate threads her arm through mine, a gesture I find uncomfortable and disturbing. I'm even more disturbed when she leans into me and kisses my cheek. Every part of me screams to move away from her. I never let my discomfort show. A smile still graces my lips, and I will myself to remain looking relaxed.

"Liam and I are expecting our first child, and, well, unfortunately, I have been experiencing a little sickness." Her hands fall onto her flat stomach.

She sees the anger in my eyes, throws back her head, and

laughs.

"Liam is *so* excited."

Turning, she places another kiss against my cheek, our eyes meet, and I am left breathless at the hard glint of hate and determination shining in their emerald depths.

Desire hits and I find myself looking forward to the end of the evening. I may not like Chrissie, but I find her intoxicating, and the thought of the coming fight is thrilling.

She turns back to Paula and John, lips pouting in a sensuous smile. "I know we promised to keep it a secret, but really, it's so difficult to keep such exciting news to ourselves. I just know that Liam was planning to tell everyone tonight. After all, our charity is in aid of the Special Care Baby Unit at York Hospital."

My hands long to close around her beautiful throat. Instead, I unwind my arm from hers. Wrapping it around her waist, I pull her to my side. My body and mind are in conflict. I want to slam myself into her until she is completely mine while my fists drive into her caramel skin and she feels the full force of my anger and dominance. I allow none of this to show on my face.

"Yes, of course, I was just waiting for everyone to gather first."

Kate laughs again.

John is hypnotized by her. He stares at her with adoring eyes.

Paula's eyes blaze and her lips become thinner. She grabs John's arm and all but pulls him to her. "What splendid news." Her voice is strained as she tries to maintain a polite appearance. "John and I, of course, are delighted for you both. Come along, dear, let's not linger. There's quite a line behind us."

Kate gives me a satisfied smile as she turns to greet the rest of our guests.

Tammy Sinclair stumbles in, having misjudged the last step into the house. To add to the disaster, her heel catches the hem of her beaded purple tulle Jovani gown. Tammy is top-heavy, and the gown's thin straps provide no support, hindered by the fact she is not wearing a bra. Her left breast makes an appearance and Tammy giggles.

With efficiency Kate moves forward steadying the giddy drunk while simultaneously pushing the breast back into the bodice of the dress.

Jeremy grabs his wife, a pained and embarrassed look on his face. He mutters, "Sorry."

Stepping forward, I air-kiss Tammy's cheeks. "It's good to see you, Tammy," I lie.

Tammy giggles again and I signal to one of the waiters. He's carrying a silver tray with crystal glasses of champagne on it.

Jeremy's lips turn into a tight smile as Tammy reaches out, snagging a flute.

"The roulette wheel is spinning," Kate suggests.

Jeremy nods. He pulls Tammy along and they make their way to the marquee, where the temporary casino is coming to life.

Tony Carlton steps forward, replacing Tammy and Jeremy. Jane Henderson adorns his side. My lips disappear in a thin line of distaste. If Tony wants to entrain garbage, that is his choice. I just wish he hadn't brought the trash to my door.

Tony fancies himself as the next Ryan Gosling, but the blue corduroy Brunello Cucinelli tux he wears and the buxom redhead on his arm fail to impress.

Jane has more flesh on show than ever before. Her

sequined pink dress, by Alice & Olive, is designed for someone much younger. Not even Jane will wear the same outfit more than once to a charity event, but with little money, her options are limited. Hence the inappropriate mini dress. In a room full of flowing gowns, the shortness of Jane's dress is noticeable.

Etiquette dictates I greet them. "Tony." We shake hands. "Jane, you look, err... lovely." Propriety does not dictate that I lean forward and air-kiss her cheeks, so I remain where I am, inclining my head.

Kate steps forward. "Please, make your way to the marquee."

Jane's lips tighten at the slight, but she makes no comment as Tony guides her into the temporary gambling venue.

Over a thousand tickets were sold for tonight's event. At two grand a ticket, plus the money exchanging hands on the gambling tables in the marquee, I will once again raise the most money for my charity. Apart from Jane, everyone present can afford to lose large amounts of cash.

Jenny and Dennis are the last of our guests to arrive. She looks radiant in an embellished long-sleeved nude Jovani gown. The simple A-line helps to slim down her thickening waist. She has made a trip to the hairdresser, and her unruly mane has been cut and restyled, dropping to her jaw in a sleek bob.

Dennis, on the other hand, looks as unkept as ever. He's wearing a black tuxedo he must have found in a charity shop. He fidgets at Jenny's side, pulling at the bow tie.

Kate opens her arms, embracing Jenny before kissing Dennis' cheek.

These events are not Dennis' scene. He prefers to stick his nose in a book. Even marking his students' papers is preferable, to Dennis. Why Jenny married him is beyond my understanding. Dennis is a plain man, with a messy appearance and no style. His job neither interests me nor brings in the money required to maintain our way of life. Jenny has married beneath herself, taking a step closer to the trash that is the middle class. My lips curl in displeasure. I have allowed Jenny her fun. Maybe it is time for Dennis to meet the end of his lifespan. At the end of the month, I will contact Jeff Green to arrange his death. It is time for Jenny to begin mixing with her peers.

"Sorry we're late, Elsie wouldn't settle." Jenny holds Kate at arm's length. "My phone has been going *wild*. You know what Paula's like." My sister turns, reaching out her hand to me while keeping a grip on Kate's arm. "Congratulations. I am bursting with excitement for you both."

Before Kate can respond, I walk forward, grabbing her arm. "Yes, well, there's more than enough time to discuss babies. Kate, our guests are waiting."

From the confident way her body sways at my side, I can tell she is pleased with tonight's performance. As this will be her only victory, I let her revel in it. At the moment, there is nothing I can do about it, and I am not about to let it spoil my night.

The marquee covers the wide expanse of the back lawn. Chandeliers hang from metal posts above our heads. Red tile flooring adds to the luxurious surroundings. The cost of tonight's event is exorbitant. Still, from the way everyone is gasping in awe and envy, it has been worth the money.

The tables are full and screams of excitement can be heard over the jazz band playing on a stage in the right corner of the marquee. Champagne flows and waiters pass silver trays of hors d'oeuvres among the guests.

The press were invited. Cameras flash and notes are taken. I have already given them the old *'It's an honour to support such a worthy cause'* speech. Kate hasn't wasted the opportunity to tell them about our impending baby. Of course, I smile at her side, and while inside I may want to the slam my fist into her stomach, to those watching I am the proud father-to-be.

The press love Kate's news, and I smile secretly to myself. Obviously, she has never heard of a miscarriage. By the time I have finished with her, she will. This is our last charity event for a while. After tonight, I no longer have to be careful where I hit her.

A reporter walks in my direction, catching my eye. "We're just about to leave."

Taking his hand, I give it a firm shake as my eyes travel over the man's suit. He must have gone to the same charity shop as Dennis. "It was good of you to come."

A representative from the hospital is here, and I nod in her direction. You can spot her a mile off, with her black high-street dress that hangs off her shoulders with little style, cut, or taste.

She waves a hand in my direction.

I turn and walk over to the roulette wheel, where Tammy is sloshing champagne over everything.

Jeremy's arm is around her waist, keeping her on the stool.

I give her another hour before she is passed out on the floor in a corner of the marquee.

Jeremy's eyes roam over the woman from the hospital, and I wonder how low some people will go.

Speaking of *low*, Tony Carlton's hands are making their way up Jane's dress. Her back is pressed hard against him.

A shout comes from the front of the house and I turn to see Henry Henderson's large form coming through the marquee's entrance. His breath is laboured.

His eyes virtually leave their sockets when he sees Jane's body twisted around Tony's. It appears, from Tony's roaming fingers digging into her naked bottom, that she has forgotten to wear any knickers.

"Jane?" Henry fades before me. His shabby trousers and thick cotton shirt highlight not only how hard his life has become, but also how much weight he has lost. Sweat trickles down his temples, and dark patches form under his armpits.

"Get stuffed, Henry." Jane manages to disentangle herself from Tony long enough to look at her husband. Her high-pitched voice sets my teeth on edge. Worse still, everyone is watching them.

"Why, Jane?" The man sounds broken.

Kate's eyes swing Henry's way. Sorrow and sadness shine from their green depths, directed at the overweight blob that is spoiling my charity event.

"I would have thought it was obvious. You promised you'd never let anything happen to Jamie, and then you lost all our money. Jamie would be alive if it weren't for you. Now do you get it?" She turns her back on Henry. Wrapping her arms around Tony's neck, she locks her lips on his.

Henry looks as though he will crumple on the spot.

Where is the security team I hired to keep the riffraff out? Someone will lose their job over this ugly performance. I have used this company on many occasions with satisfying results. Tonight, they have let me down for the first and last time.

Once this scene is over, I will also speak to Tony about leaving the trash at home. If he wants to slum it, that is fine, but this is the last time he will bring it to my door.

Chapter Twenty-One

KATE

Henry bursts through the opening of the marquee and people turn their attention away from the tables to watch. Liam's eyes scan the crowd, looking for security.

Jane's hurtful words and the obscene display she is putting on with Tony are dreadful.

Tony really should know better than to bring Jane here.

I have no love for Jane, or the terrible things she is saying and doing to hurt Henry. While Jamie's death is unfortunate, it isn't Henry's fault. Does she care so little that she's willing to rip at Henry's heart further? It makes me wonder if she has a heart.

Despite Liam's dislike of Jane, their cold temperaments are a perfect match.

Jane turns her back on her husband and flings herself at

Tony, who is only too happy to accept Jane's sexual advances.

Henry's face crumples.

"Henry." Laying a gentle hand on his shoulder, I break the spell Jane and Tony's display has on him.

"Come, let's go somewhere quiet. You don't want to be here."

Henry doesn't say a word as I lead him out of the marquee. It's hard to talk when your heart is breaking into tiny pieces.

The living room is the farthest place from the crowd I can think of to take Henry.

A man in a white shirt and florescent armband comes forward. I shake my head at him, and he stays where he is.

Jake appears at my side and we walk into the house in silence. The only sound are my shoes clicking out a slow steady beat across the marble floor.

Moonlight pours into the living room. Without stopping to turn on the light, I lead Henry to the plush Boston sofa.

Jake stops at the other side of the sofa, looking down at us.

"She's right, you know. I killed our son."

My heart squeezes tight within my chest at his words. I look up at Jake, our eyes meeting in perfect understanding. Liam is a bastard.

"No, Henry, you didn't. Jamie would have died no matter how much money you had. Jane's hurting and taking it out on you. I'm sure that when she calms down, she'll see that you had nothing to do with the death of your son." Personally, I am unsure Jane will *ever* understand.

"Henry," I urge him.

He looks up at me and I squirm at the pain shimmering within the depths of his eyes. My discomfort is heightened by the knowledge that Liam is ultimately responsible for it.

Jane may blame their son's death on their lack of money, due to Henry's poor investments, but some things cannot be fixed with a fistful of paper with the queen's head on it.

Henry lets out a sob and Jake hands me a box of tissues. I pass them to Henry, my arm resting on his shoulder as I try to comfort him. There is nothing I can say to make his pain disappear. His voice is nothing but a broken mutter as he continues blaming himself for the loss of his home, wife, and child. Sweat licks at his skin and his colouring takes on a sickly shade.

"Henry." My hands shake as I push at him, trying to get his attention. "Henry…"

His eyes bulge, his fingers clutch at his chest, and he rocks forward. I look at Jake for help as Henry topples off the sofa onto the floor, taking me with him. My scream cuts through the quiet room. We land, in a tangle of limbs, on the carpet. Henry's arms fly around him. His body convulses.

Jake grabs my arm, pulling me away from Henry before he hurts me.

I want to yell at Jake to see to Henry and leave me alone.

As I come to my knees, I notice the phone plastered to Jake's ear. His face is scrunched up as he listens to what the person on the other end is saying. Time seems conflicted, speeding up as Henry thrashes on the floor and slowing down as I look at Jake. I feel trapped and completely useless.

The sound of an ambulance echoes around the room, the siren breaking through the laughter and music filtering in from the marquee. Flashing blue lights dance round the room, and two paramedics come running in, along with a man from the security firm.

Everything seems to be happening at once. Jake and I

stand back allowing the men from the ambulance to take care of Henry. I watch as they wheel Henry out of the house and into the ambulance. The doors slam shut, and I know with absolute certainty that Henry will die before the night is over.

Henry's world has splintered into a mass of tiny pieces, and sometimes a person can't live in the wreckage that is left behind. Death is the preferable option, and Henry's heart is willing to provide the final solution.

"You know, Jake, I just don't understand Liam. Why did he need to break Henry? What type of person revels in the destruction of another?" Without thought, my hand rests on my belly.

Jake lays his gnarled hand on mine. "I've watched him for so long, watched him change, and still, lass, I have no answers for you. But know this – you don't need to worry about that baby you're carrying. I will ensure Liam does nothing to hurt it. Will you be able to love it?"

I look into Jake's eyes. They show a lifetime of regret. "My fight for my baby has already started."

I think about Liam and the anger lurking behind those sharp blue eyes, aware that payback for my earlier performance over our baby news is inevitable. I am not sure how Jake will be able to stop him. Still, I have no regrets.

"I can't kill my baby, no matter how they were made, or who their father is. It's not their fault. I would never have chosen to have Liam's child, but, to me, life is life, and this baby is still a part of me." A slight smile on my lips, I realize how much I am capable of loving this child. "I love my baby... because it will never be Liam's. I'll make sure of that."

Jake nods and we stand watching the ambulance leave, our faces bathed in blue light.

As the ambulance disappears from view, I turn and walk

back into the house. "I need to let Jane know about Henry. She is still his wife."

"I'll get Junior to bring a car round, in case she wants to go to the hospital," Jake calls as I enter the marquee.

The noise that had been a gentle tease now shouts at me. Poor Henry. Life has continued, and it appears no one has given him another thought, caring little about the broken man. I dare say that none of them care about each other.

Whoops of joy ring out as the roulette wheel turns, and laughter fills the tent.

Liam raises a questioning eyebrow, a champagne flute dangling from his hand.

"Henry has had a heart attack. I don't think he's going to make it."

Satisfaction falls across his lips before he can hide it.

Sadness fills me. Liam lives in a cold world.

I walk away from him. Let him rejoice, I want no part in it.

Jane is downing a glass of champagne reaching for another as I approach her. She raises the flute in mock salute, pouring the contents down her neck. Perhaps her earlier cold display was an illusion.

Tony is nowhere to be seen. That is love-them-and-leave-them Tony.

"Henry's had a heart attack."

Jane looks at me as though I have grown an extra head. "So?"

I close my eyes and breathe deep, steadying my anger.

"Jane, I don't think Henry is going to survive it."

"Quite fitting then, isn't it?"

"Jane, I know you're hurting right now, but think about it. You may never get another chance to talk to Henry." There is a need to breakdown her walls and make her understand the enormity of what is happening to Henry, to her.

Jane sets down her empty glass. "Like I care."

"Maybe you don't right now, but at some point, you might, and for that reason alone, I think it might be worth saying your goodbyes."

I'm not sure Jane will get to the hospital in time to say what she needs to say to Henry, but it has to be worth trying. "Jane, I think Henry's dying."

She stares at me as my words penetrate her brain. Her eyes fill with tears as her hand flies to her lips. "What have I done?"

Death is a rude awaking. "Nothing that can't be forgiven."

"I've been so horrible."

My hand touches her arm. "Come on, I'll take you to the hospital."

Jenny looks at me, concern pinching her brows together, as I lead Jane out of the marquee.

I shake my head at her and continue walking.

Our heels click on the cold marble floor as Jane and I make our way through the house.

Jake Junior is standing next to the Bentley, waiting for us. "Would you like me to drive, Mrs. Thornton?"

"Please."

Junior opens the back door of the Bentley, and I help Jane settle herself in the back of the car.

She raises a hand as I start following her inside. "I'd rather do this on my own."

I nod, stepping away.

Junior runs around to the other side.

"Be careful. I know you need to get her there quickly, Jake

Junior, but take it steady."

Junior raises his hand to his head in salute as he climbs into the car.

I stand there, staring into the darkness, long after it has disappeared from view. The stars shine down on me, barely visible against the light flooding the house and grounds. "Please get there in time," I whisper into the night.

Silent, I walk back to the marquee and our guests, wishing I could leave them to their fun, but knowing Liam would flip if I did. Things have worked out perfectly for him.

As I walk through the front door and close it behind me, Jenny is standing in the hall near the stairs. Without a word, she walks over and opens her arms, and we hug each other. Tears threaten to spill down my cheeks.

"Better?" Jenny asks.

I nod. "You're the best, Jenny."

"And don't you forget it."

I laugh at her as she threads her arm through mine.

"Come on, Kate, there's orange juice to be drunk. Actually, you look as though you could do with a good stiff orange juice. I'll get them to leave the bits in for you."

If it weren't for Jenny, I know I would struggle to walk back into that tent without falling apart.

Chapter Twenty-Two

LIAM

The marquee stands empty and I walk around the still gambling-tables, trailing my fingers on the wooden frames. It is four a.m., and the last of our guests left over an hour ago. My satisfaction grows spilling into the tent and following me around.

Despite Henry Henderson's sudden and irksome appearance, the night went well. Even better, I will never have to experience another visit from that overweight excuse for a man. I have been informed that Henry died on his way to the hospital. An element I did not see coming, but a welcome one, nonetheless.

I turn at the sound of rustling fabric and watch as Kate walks into the marquee. Lines pull at her eyes. She looks tired.

"I'm going to bed. I take it you don't need me for anything else?"

I look down at the blackjack table. "You might think you're clever, telling everyone about the baby. But don't think you can outsmart me, Kate."

If she wants to play games, she'd better get used to the consequences.

"No, Liam, I wasn't being clever. I was protecting my baby."

My eyes meet hers. She reminds me of a lioness watching her enemy sneak ever closer to her cubs. Kate doesn't know how beautiful she looks as she stands there in the white figure-hugging dress, green fire blazing from her eyes.

I walk over to her. My fingers trailing along the baize on the betting tables.

She turns to leave, and I catch her arm.

"Where do you think you're going?" Anger and desire vibrate in my voice.

"I'm going to bed, Liam." Her eyes linger where my fingers grip her.

"You don't go until I tell you that you can."

Pulling her to me, I place my mouth on hers. She tries to twist her head away. My fingers grip her jaw digging into her flesh, forcing her to accept my kiss.

My teeth bite at her ear. "It's payback time, Kate, and I will take what I am owed."

"No!"

Sensing her fear, I tighten my grip, pushing her onto the wooden frame of one of the betting tables.

"Oh, but I think so." My hand runs down her body, digging into the fabric of her dress, catching hold of her skin.

I'm not stupid enough to believe Kate's fear is directed at me. It is for that *thing* she carries in her belly. Like a parasite, it sucks at her body, taking its nutrients from her, selfish and thoughtless. Her body will change, and whether I grow tired of it or not, she has no right to no longer be the beautiful, svelte creature that stands before me.

I have forgiven her, her background, willing to overlook it because of the unusual exotic creature she is. I've taken her body and made it mine. I will not let anything take it from me. That baby would take my Kate. I will not, cannot, allow that thing inside her to live.

"Let go of her, Liam."

Jake stands in the entrance of the marquee and my fingers fall from Kate as I stare at him.

"Go to bed, lass. You'll find the lock has been replaced on your bedroom door. I suggest you use it."

Kate nods at Jake as she slithers away from the betting table.

My hand shoots out to grab her, but all I catch is air as she runs out of the tent.

Confused, I look at Jake. "Don't interfere, old man. This is between me and my wife."

Jake has never meddled in my business before, and it unnerves me that he is doing so now. My heart goes cold and I begin severing one of the last links I have to my past. Jake will never interfere again.

"Liam, that isn't your wife."

Caught off guard, my mouth hangs open.

Just what has the bitch been telling him? I begin wondering who else she has been talking to. Obviously, the threat I made against her husband and child wasn't enough. The stupid bitch! Did she not realise I was serious? Well, she will soon find out.

I slam my fist on the blackjack table. "Again, old man, I'll ask you not to interfere."

Jake moves closer and I hold my ground as his old bones creak their way across the floor.

"I've watched you destroy everything, lad. I've never said a thing, but the child that poor lass is carrying deserves to live. It could, quite possibly, be your own salvation."

I raise my eyebrows at him. "I don't need saving, Jake. What I need is for you to go back to tending the garden and leave me alone."

Jake stops in front of me. "You think that because my body is failing, my mind has gone as well. These eyes see everything. I've known since you brought that poor lass home that she wasn't Kate."

Shaking my head, I look at Jake. "I haven't got a clue what you're talking about. It sounds like the mumblings of an old brain that has stopped working."

Jake draws himself as straight as his arthritic body will allow and pulls a piece of paper out of his trouser pocket. Slapping it on the table, he looks at me. "Don't play your games with me, lad. I know the truth."

The skin on my cheeks pulse. I pick up the photograph and look at Kate and Chrissie in their pretty dresses, so alike, and yet so different. They might be mirror images of each other, but I can tell them apart. It is their eyes that separate them. That's where the differences lie.

"Where did you get this?" I look at Jake, aware that I have been caught.

"Kate gave it to me, a long time ago. She was scared that, if you ever found out, you would use it against her."

My Kate wasn't as docile as I thought she was.

"I've watched you as you dominated and tried to break that lass, watched you until the spark of happiness died in her eyes. I won't stand by and watch you do the same thing to her sister. You leave that poor girl and her baby alone. If I were you, I would be grateful that she is prepared to love that baby of yours."

Anger simmers inside me. How has this happened? Even when Kate told me she was dying I found a way around it. I will not fail. Failure is for the likes of the Henry Hendersons of this world.

I walk past Jake. Our arms touch. "You have no idea what you have done, old man."

Jake snorts. "I know *exactly* what I have done, and what I am willing to do to protect that baby of yours. The choice is yours, Liam. Take the time to contemplate the life that grows in that lass's belly. It could change you, make you more of a person."

The old man doesn't get it. I don't *want* to change. I like the person I have become.

Tomorrow – or, rather, later today – I will contact Jeff Green. It is time I showed Jake just what I am willing to do, and how far I will go to keep what is mine.

First on my hit list for Jeff Green is Jake. His death will be quick. Jake's Russian story is about to catch up with him. Second is Chrissie's husband, Simon. I will leave her daughter orphaned, with no hope of adoption. I will make sure of it.

Chapter Twenty-Three

LIAM

The red Ferrari glistens in the sun. It was my 'bonus' purchase that I rewarded myself with when Henry signed the contract.

The car's blood-red body beckons me. The colour takes on a new meaning – when I come home, I'll find Jake dead.

Yesterday, I gave Jake's details to Jeff Green, putting out a hit on him. The old man is the only person I have ever loved. After last night, I know I can no longer afford such luxuries in my life.

Chrissie's husband, Simon, is due to meet an unfortunate end later in the week. It fits nicely with the man's schedule to leave it until Wednesday. The quick turnaround will cost me double Jeff Green's normal payment, but this situation warrants it.

I've made sure Simon's death will hit the front pages of

the newspaper. A stabbing so brutal it will shock the local community. Chrissie needs to understand *exactly* what she is dealing with. Maybe then she will book herself into a clinic and get rid of the baby before it becomes too late, and we can return to some normality.

Chrissie gone and my Kate back, this time for good.

My ability to take care of the baby matter myself is somewhat reduced because Jake replaced the lock on Kate's bedroom door. The bitch is still locked in there now. She'd better enjoy it while she can. By tonight, my balance of power will be restored.

Sliding into the leather seat, I turn the key and the engine thunders to life. Tyres squeal as I put my foot down and drive onto the main road. My decision to put the hit out on Jake has not been an easy one, and it bothers me that I have been forced into making the decision. Still, I can't afford for Jake to interfere in my business as he did last night. I don't understand why he chose to side with that bitch and her parasite of a baby. The speech about the child being my salvation was sheer stupidity talking.

I am true to myself, taking what I want and destroying those that have the audacity to try and surpass their breeding and class, or that get in my way. Most people hide their true natures, even from themselves. Not me. I know what I am, and I like what I see. Some may call me evil, but I like to think of myself as a realist.

The scenery becomes a blur as I increase my speed. I take the next corner a little too tightly. The scent of burning rubber drifts through the open window. My heart beats quick in my chest from the rush of adrenalin, and I smile as I accelerate.

The Ferrari eagerly responds, flying forward like a bullet freed from the barrel of a gun. The engine roars and the tyres eat at the tarmac.

A tractor pulls out in front of me as I hit another bend in the road. Slamming down on the brake, I grit my teeth, my arms locking as I fight for control. At the speed I am travelling, the gap between me and the tractor isn't sufficient for me to stop in time. I swerve and the Ferrari squeals, rubber burns, and this time I don't smile.

Losing my fight for control, the car spins three hundred sixty degrees, and I grip the steering wheel knuckles turning white. My muscles are taut, my hands tremble from the pressure. Sweat lines my forehead and trickles down my back. The car slams into the tractor, the impact throwing me forward. Too late, I recognise that I should have used the seat belt.

The crunch of glass and scream of metal follow the collision between car and tractor. Pain shoots up my body and I lie there, semi-conscious, wondering what has happened.

I hear the tread of boots and relief floods through me. I manage to tilt my head toward the coming footsteps. A man's head appears to my right as he leans in.

"You don't look so good, Mr. Thornton."

I look the man over, unable to recall seeing him before. Yet, he knows my name, so we have met at some point it time.

Dark brown, almost black eyes stare down at me. His head is bald, which accentuates his sharp, jutting jaw. The broadness of his shoulders tells me he is a tall man. Muscles bulge across his arms. He's a man that likes to work with weights.

His clothes are High Street – black jeans and a white t-shirt. No, I can't imagine ever having anything to do with him.

While I am confused about how he knows my name, I am

not about to be discourteous to him. He is, after all, the only one around who can help me.

"I've crashed my car." I hate it when people state the obvious, but my head hurts, and I am losing feeling in my arms and legs. Therefore, I can forgive myself for being obvious on this occasion.

"Yeah, I can see that." The man bends and his legs click. "You're dying, Mr. Thornton."

My eyes widen in fear. I don't want to die. I have far too much to do. I haven't put out the hit on Dennis yet. Kate is still pregnant. I need to review my position on Pete Townsend and teach Tony a lesson. Far too much for me to do to die. I don't like loose ends. They are an irritation that requires stamping out.

"I thought you might appreciate a car accident. After all, it has always been a favourite of yours."

What is the man babbling about?

My breath catches in the back of my throat. "Jeff Green?"

"In the flesh, Mr. Thornton. I wanted to meet you before you died. It seems only right. After all, you've brought a lot of business my way over the years."

I knit my brow, unable to understand what is going on. Why is Jeff Green here? The man is paid well, and I have never been late on a payment. Something is off.

"Why?" It is strange how a three-letter word can carry so much weight.

"Simple, Mr. Thornton. You put out a hit on the wrong man."

"Simon Sanders?" How does Chrissie's husband and Jeff Green know each other? What is their connection?

"Nope. Jake McCloud." Jeff's voice has a rasp to it, like he has spent his life chewing on sandpaper.

"Jake. Jake put out a hit on me?" Disbelief resonates in my voice. *How can he afford a hitman?*

"Nope." Jeff grins at my confusion, revealing white, even teeth. "Jake saved my family and me from a house fire forty years ago. I owe him my life, and my family's. That's the kind of thing a man never forgets."

The Russian story is real!

Sweat lines my skin and I acknowledge that I am going to die.

I don't want to die.

I lick my shaking lips. "Look, I didn't know. How about we just forget about the hit on Jake? I'm sure we can come to some arrangement. I'll wire the money to you for the inconvenience."

Jeff shakes his head. "Sorry, Mr. Thornton, no can do. You're bleeding out. By now, you'll have lost feeling in your arms and legs. Your heart is pumping your blood out onto the upholstery of that flashy car of yours. You must be feeling really tired. Bet you'd like to close your eyes."

"No. I can't die." But Jeff is right. My eyelids are getting heavier, and it is difficult to concentrate, to focus on the real issue here.

"What about Simon Sanders?" I want Chrissie to suffer. She deserves it.

"Sorry, Mr. Thornton. I don't take money from dead men, and as you haven't paid yet... I'm sure you can understand my position." Jeff stands, his legs clicking back into place.

"No..." Darkness pulls at me, and I am starting to feel so cold, so very cold.

I can hear Jeff whistling as he walks away, and in the dim recesses of my mind I begin wondering if this is really it. Is there such a thing as an afterlife? I have never believed in

God, or the inner makings of a man that people refer to as a soul. Now, as my life slips away, I want to know that this isn't the end. That, in some way, I will survive this.

Born again, into a new life, maybe? I don't care. I just don't want this to be the end.

Panic fills me, and my eyes fly open. I am alone, and I realise I don't want to die alone. But, then, we don't always get what we want.

Jake is alive, Simon will get to live, Jenny will live out her days married to someone beneath her breeding, and Chrissie is still pregnant.

I have had bad days before, but this one… This one has to be the worst.

My eyelids close, and my breath shudders in my chest.

There is no coming back from this.

I wonder if I will see my Kate, meet her in whatever place she went to when she died. It seems we were both destined to die too young.

Chapter Twenty-Four

JESSICA

The bedroom fills with the sound of my screams and I long for this to be over, for the pain to stop. I am eight hours into my labour, and I have yet to hold one baby in my arms, never mind two.

Sweat drips from my forehead and my breath comes in gasps. The pain subsides for a brief second, and I pant, ready for the next wave of contractions to hit. It feels like a decade ago since my water broke and my contractions started.

"One more push, Jess, you're nearly there," Charles encourages me.

I don't respond. His encouragement and upbeat mood is condescending and irritating. Eight hours of labour can make you tense, and your tolerance evaporates to nothing.

Another contraction hits and I scream again, reconsidering my decision for a home birth. A little late for this, I know, but it helps me refocus and to not take it out on Charles, who I have wanted to punch several times since I went into labour. The perky excitement radiating off of him adds to my peeved attitude.

My hair and nightie stick to my skin. My legs are spread and the midwife assesses the situation. Like Charles, the midwife is perky beyond belief. She keeps telling me I am, 'Nearly there, only a few more pushes.' Each time she says this, I feel the need to kick her. Not that I do.

While she says I am 'nearly there,' a baby has yet to appear, and I'm beginning to question how *nearly* there is.

Charles tried to sway my decision for a home birth once we found out I was having twins. I do not consider myself a stubborn person, and yet, on the question of birthing locations, he was unable to change my mind.

So why did I refuse to listen to the professionals and remain steadfast in having my babies at home? It all seems rather silly now, but I wanted our babies' introduction to this world to be in the place where Charles and I had first been allowed to love each other.

I am a romantic, always have been. I see no need to change now.

Besides, Charles is a doctor. A doctor in a different field than childbirth, but a doctor is a doctor. The human anatomy doesn't change, just the circumstances. I haven't mentioned my simplistic view on doctors and the medical profession to Charles. His eyebrows would hit his hairline. He would also break into a lecture about specialist fields and whatnot. In secret, I think this is the problem with the whole medical profession. They over-complicate things. Not that I am going to share this view with Charles, either.

A baby's cry merges with my screams, and I flop against

the pillows, watching a multitude of wonderful expressions filter across Charles' face.

"She's gorgeous. Look, Jess." Charles takes our baby from the midwife and hands her to me.

My eyes fill with tears, and I smile as my irritation falls away as I look at the tiny baby in my arms.

"We made this."

I look at Charles and see so much love shining in the depths of his hazel eyes.

"She has your nose." My fingers trail light along her cheek, and she scrunches up her face, lips pouting.

"God help her," Charles chuckles.

"I like your nose. It's cute."

I hand our daughter back to her daddy as another contraction hits and our second baby begins its move for freedom. Our daughter cries with her mummy. Twenty minutes later, her brother's cries join ours.

Tears roll down my cheeks as I hold our babies. Soft lips kiss my sweaty forehead and Charles sits on the bed next to me.

The midwife stands at the end of the bed. "We should get them washed."

I smile at her, thinking that she has the best job in the world. Despite wanting to kick her earlier.

Charles picks up our daughter and the midwife takes our son.

"Get some rest. We'll be back in a minute, and I'll help get you cleaned up."

My fingers trail along Charles' face as he kisses my lips. "I love you," I whisper.

Lying back against the pillows, I smile up at the ceiling with contentment, congratulating myself on doing something amazing. I gave birth to the most beautiful babies I have ever seen. Of course, there is a part of me that recognises most new mums feel this way, but I don't care. My babies were made with love and born into a world of love, and not all children are lucky enough to have that.

* * *

I wake sometime later to the hungry cries of my daughter. I don't know how I know that it is my daughter crying, but either instinct or mothers love tells me she's the unhappy one.

Charles passes her to me, and she attaches her mouth to my breast. Not to be left out, our son begins crying. Charles helps as I juggle and rearrange them so both babies can feed.

Charles laughs. "Christine is definitely your daughter."

"And Jacob has his dad's appetite."

"Can you manage?"

"Don't worry so much, they're doing fine."

"I'm so proud of you." His voice is low, almost a whisper.

I lean my face into his cupped hand as he touches my skin, kissing his palm.

My thoughts drift to Chrissie. I'm aware that I am no longer in a position to find her, not with Liam around. "Do you think Chrissie would understand?"

"I'm sure she would. She would want you to be safe and happy, even if that meant there's no possibility of you two being reunited."

I nod. "I've been doing a lot of thinking about her lately. I think it's these two that've done it."

"I know, Jess. I just wish there was another way."

"It's OK. I know there isn't. I'm just being melancholy."

I am not giving up on the hope of being reunited with my sister,

I tell myself. Someday, should things change – maybe when Liam is settled with someone else, or, better yet, dead – then I will be free to find Chrissie and tell her how much she means to me.

Hope sent me Charles, and he gave me two beautiful babies to love, and a world filled with happiness.

No, I am not going to give up on hope, no matter how long I have to wait.

Chapter Twenty-Five

CHRISSIE

Liam is dead.

After all these months of living in hell with him, I can't believe it. Part of me still expects him to walk through the front door, to ostracise me further from the person I was.

I take a deep breath and place a gentle hand on my swollen belly. The babies move under my fingers.

The funeral was a lavish affair, as per his will. While strange, I am not surprised that Liam organised his own funeral in advance, taking control right to the end. He would have been pleased with the turnout. Tammy even managed to remain sober until after the church service.

The only emotion I feel is relief.

Tears roll down Jenny's cheeks and she leans into Dennis for support. Liam doesn't deserve her love. They left Elsie in the care of Dennis' parents.

I stand at his graveside, detached and aloof, unsure how to feel as earth and flowers are thrown onto the wooden casket. When they lower the coffin, part of me wants to demand that they open it so I can make sure Liam is inside, that he has not slithered off somewhere. But I remain unmoving and silent.

I have entertained Liam's so-called friends for the last time. Liam's death released Tony from his restraint, and he wastes no time in coming on to me as we leave Liam's coffin to be covered in earth. My green eyes stare at him, and I pour all my hate into that stare, not saying a word.

He coughs, mutters, and walks away.

These people act like toddlers wearing the skins of an adult. I neither need nor want any part of their world.

After the service, we retire to Whitegates, its shiny white paintwork a contrast to the many black outfits of the mourners.

When everyone leaves, I remain standing in the living room as shadows spread across the plush carpeted floor, and I cry.

My tears are not for Liam. Never for him, but for a life that, even now, I can never have back.

Simon remains lost to me, and it hurts, it hurts so much.

The day after I received the news about Liam's death, I drove to the house Simon and I shared. Sitting in the car a slight distance away, I watched, waiting for Simon and Imogen to come home. At the time, I had intended to tell Simon what happened, but as my hand rested on my swollen belly, I knew I couldn't. I couldn't do it to him.

How could I ask him – knowing how this life inside me was created – to not only accept that I was raped repeatedly by Liam, but to accept his children and not blame them for their father's sins? I battled with myself over this issue as I sat in the car. Of course, I am aware that I could give him the choice, but would it be fair of me to do so? Over time, Simon will build a new life and find someone else to love. While the thought tears me apart, I know I have to let him go, no matter the cost to myself.

I have been with another man and allowed that man to touch me. The fact I never wanted Liam to rape me doesn't change what happened, and I feel like I have let both myself and Simon down. I am so angry – at myself, at Liam – that logic doesn't stand a chance of entering into the argument.

I didn't wait for Simon and Imogen to come home. I told myself it was better if I remained distant from their lives.

"You OK?" Jenny comes and sits down next to me, folding her legs under her.

Her hair has grown to her shoulders and frames her face in a mass of frizzy curls.

I place a hand over my large belly, fingers brushing the soft cream fabric of my cashmere sweater. Neither of us wears makeup. Liam would have a fit if he could see the pair of us, all comfy-clothed and not a designer label in sight. I can almost hear his voice muttering about 'high-street trash' and it makes me smile.

"I'm fine." I say, tucking a strand of hair behind my ear.

"No, you're not, I can tell."

Patting her knee, I smile at her. "You worry too much."

"Someone's got to."

In the early stages of mourning her brother's death, Jenny clung to me like I was her lifeline. We sat like statues at the reading of the will, gripped within an icy storm as we listened to Liam's demands. More revelations rolled our way. Clearing out the study removed any pretence of brotherly love on

Liam's part. The contents of his safe included his to-do list, which was also a hit list. Poor Dennis. The information hit Jenny the hardest. I already knew what Liam was capable of.

Though my bank accounts remain in my sister's name, at home in Whitegates I am Chrissie once more. It is good to have my name back, and be me again, and to not pretend to be my sister. The loss of my name while Liam was alive made me aware how important a name is. A person's name is a vital part of who they are. To lose it is like losing a part of oneself, of one's identity.

Liam left most of his estate to me. Well, to Kate. I have two babies to think about now, so I accepted the money, the house, and the responsibility for those I employ – Jake and Jake Junior, though I don't see them as employees so much as family.

I have left Liam's old life behind. His so-called friends have fallen away like rats running from daylight.

My first job as owner of Whitegates was to terminate Mrs. Jones' employment. Whether I liked her or not was immaterial. She smelled of stale fags. In my present condition, waves of nausea hit every time she got close, or when I happened to walk into a room, she had just vacated. However, if I am honest, a big part of giving her the heave-ho was because I *didn't* like her. Liam did, and that was a good enough reason for me to get rid of her.

Together, Jenny and I have remodelled the house. It has been our therapy. We have taken it from a heartless domain and transformed it into something quite splendid. The expensive artwork is gone, along with the antiquities. All auctioned off to someone who will appreciate them.

It has given me a sense of satisfaction to strip away everything Liam ever cared about and replace it with a soft, homey style of love. The house is no longer soulless. Photographs of Elsie hang from some of the walls. Family images can be seen everywhere you look. Even Jake and Jake Junior's photographs sit on the side unit in the living room.

Liam's study has become a playroom for Elsie. The wall with the small window was removed and now large patio doors bring in the sunlight. Fairy stickers cover the bright-yellow paintwork.

The sofa we are sitting on is littered with animal cushions, and Elsie's contented gurgles fill the room, as she plays with the toys scattered across the floor.

Jake walks into the room, wearing his blue overalls, and Elsie screams with joy, crawling toward him like a tornado. As she gets closer to him, she stops standing on her wobbly legs. With the confidence of knowing Jake will protect her, she launches herself at him.

Jake's old bones are put to the test and he lurches forward, scooping the squealing child to him. Jenny and I laugh at the two of them as Jake tries to exercise some control over the wiggling child in his arms.

"Come on, lass, you've got to give an old man a chance."

Elsie giggles, her fingers latching on to his snowy-white hair.

Jenny stands, reaching over for Elsie placing her back in the middle of the carpet and the hundreds of toys sitting there. Pressing down on a teddy's red paw, he springs to life and sings. Refocused, Elsie grabs the bear and begins chewing on his ear.

"You know, she reminds me of a certain young gardener I have, a very distracted gardener."

"Jake Junior spending too much time with a certain automobile?" I enquire innocently.

"You know he is," Jake grumbles as he sits in a high-backed chair.

I shrug. "It makes him happy, and what did I want with the car?"

"Oh, yes, I'll give you that, lass, it makes him very happy. He should be out dating a girl, not lusting after a car."

"It's an Aston Martin, Jake, it deserves to be lusted after," Jenny says as she flops back onto the sofa.

"Not when he should be cleaning the leaves off the lawn. These old bones of mine hate the damp. Winter is coming and they know it, otherwise I would pick them up myself."

I shake my head. "No, that's not Jake Junior's fault, it's mine. I asked him to leave the leaves for the hedgehogs."

Jake looks at me like I have lost my mind.

I sigh. "They need the leaves to insulate themselves against the cold. A tidy garden is not always a happy garden, Jake."

He huffs, and I know that is the only response I am going to get.

The doorbell rings and we look at each other. No one moves.

"I'll get it," I say as I inch to the edge of the sofa.

"You stay there, I'll get it." Jenny looks at her watch. "It's time for Elsie's nap, anyway."

Once Whitegates was transformed into a home, Jenny, Dennis, and Elsie moved in, taking up residence in what we refer to as 'the north wing'. The place is more than large enough to accommodate our expanding family. My rooms are on the west side of the house.

"I'd better go too. The garden won't tend itself, especially since I seem to be a gardener down at the moment."

I laugh at Jake's retreating back.

The teddy dangles from Elsie's hand as Jenny picks her up and walks to the door. Her eyes are already heavy, and the teddy falls to the floor as her head rests on her mum's shoulder.

"I'll get the door, lass. You see to the little one."

"Thanks, Jake," Jenny calls.

Sliding off the sofa, onto the floor, I start picking up the toys, placing them in the bright painted toy box. Footsteps echo on the marble floor and I turn, my arms full of toys, wondering what Jenny has forgotten. My mouth falls open and the toys tumble to the floor. Tears sting the back of my eyes. I blink, but she is still standing there. My hands shake and the tears fall down my face. It feels like a dream, but I know I am awake. And, best of all, she is here with me.

Before I can say anything, she runs over, dropping to the floor next to me and throwing her arms around me. I hold onto her as tight as my swelling stomach allows, and together we cry.

My sister has come home.

Kate leans back, brushing the hair from my face. "I thought I'd never see you again."

"Me neither." I cry into her shoulder.

I hope Liam can see us in whatever place his soul was taken to, and that he is having a good rant about us. He is unable to control us anymore. We are finally free.

Kate holds out her hand, pulling me off the floor, and together we sit on the sofa, our hands clinging to each other. Staring at her, I notice how happy and relaxed she looks.

"I saw your photo in the newspaper. It was while you were at Liam's funeral. I rang Jake, and he told me what had happened. Chrissie, I'm so sorry, I didn't know he knew about you. Had I known what Liam would do, I'd never have left."

Her guilt cloaks her in sadness and I wrap my arms around her. Liam has done enough to both of us. I am not prepared to let him touch us even in death.

Placing a finger on her lips, I shake my head. "Don't. You had a chance at happiness, and you took it. I can't blame you for that. What happened to me had nothing to do with you and everything to do with Liam."

"Thank you for not hating me."

"I couldn't. We're sisters, Kate."

A baby cries out, and I know it isn't Elsie.

Kate smiles. "That's Christine. She's probably wondering where I've gone."

A man walks into the room, a screaming baby in his arms. His black hair tickles the tops of his ears, and his skin is tanned.

Jake appears with another baby.

"Sorry, love, Christine wasn't happy about being left out. I'm telling you, she gets more like her mother every day."

Kate snorts, holding out her arms. "You mean more like her dad."

My hand rests on my belly as I look at Kate's twins. One dressed in blue, the other pink.

Christine stops her crying as she sits on her mother's knees, openly staring at me.

"Why don't you say hello to your Auntie Chrissie?" Kate smiles down at her daughter.

"Hello, Christine. It's very nice to meet you." I take her small hand and give it a little shake.

Christine gurgles at me, her chubby fingers pulling on Kate's ponytail.

Both babies have a thick mop of black hair and green eyes.

Their skin looks as though it has been kissed by the sun.

Jake lowers the baby boy onto his knee as he sits down in his high-backed chair again. "If Jake Junior doesn't leave that car alone, I think I may have found his replacement."

We laugh and the baby joins in, his fists and legs bouncing.

Jenny walks into the room. Her eyes flicker from Kate to me, and she comes to an abrupt stop. "Oh, oh, oh, K-Kate?"

Kate walks over to Jenny, balancing Christine on her hip, and gives her a hug. "I go by Jessica now."

"I-I can't b-believe it," Jenny stutters as Kate leads her over to the sofa.

Jessica. I have to remember to start calling her Jessica *now*, I tell myself.

"Isn't it amazing?" I nudge Jenny.

Jenny nods. "You bet. But… How?"

I incline my head at Jake. "We have that conniving old man in the chair over there to thank for this."

Jake looks offended. "I have no idea what you mean, lass."

Like hell he doesn't.

"Well, I think we should all give a big thank-you to the conniving old man." Jenny winks at Jake.

"Less of the 'old', lass, the mind's still young."

Jake Junior walks into the room and stops as he looks from me to Jessica. "Wow! That water must have packed more of a punch than I thought."

"Are you sure it was water you were drinking?" I ask him with a grin.

"Definitely water. I want to take my car for a spin later."

Jake snorts, sending a pained look my way. "Come on, lad. As you're here, I might as well see if I can get some work out of you today."

"I don't know what you mean." Junior scratches his head, a confused expression falling across his face.

"Don't play the innocent with me, lad. It's flowers you need to be attending to, not some bit of metal."

"It's not a bit of metal, it's an Aston Martin!"

"Might as well be a tin can for all I care." Jake shuffles to the door. "Charles, it's good to see you. Thank you for looking after her." He hands the baby to his dad as he approaches Junior. "Come on, lad, let's go get some work done." Taking his flat cap from his overall pocket, Jake swipes at Junior.

Junior laughs as he follows Jake out of the room.

Jenny pats Jessica's arm. "So, come on, tell me everything."

I watch Jessica as she tells us about her and Charles and their plan for her to leave Liam, and how scared she was that Liam would find out. Her eyes light up as she speaks about their house in Portree and I love seeing her looking so happy.

As I listen, I can't help thinking that my sister is the bravest person I have ever met. Having lived with Liam for just shy of a year, I know he would never have allowed her to divorce him.

Charles looks across at Jenny. "I'm sorry, Jenny. It must be hard hearing all this about Liam. He was, after all, your brother."

"I've had quite a tough time since Liam died. I can't believe all the things he's done. It's just horrible. For my own sanity, I've come to the conclusion that my brother died long before his body did."

Sadness clouds the room, and I make the decision to stop it in its tracks. "Come on, this is supposed to be a happy reunion. We should be celebrating. Now, someone give this beached whale a hand up so we can start our celebration in style. I've got the keys to the wine cellar, and I know for certain there's some rather swish champagne down there."

Jenny giggles as she pulls me off the sofa.

"You're right." Jessica stands up. "Come on, let's raid the fridge and get this party started. Is Mrs. Jones still about?"

I laugh. In some ways, we are remarkably similar. "Nope, she's gone. She smelled bad and, in my present state, that isn't a good thing. Besides, I don't think she ever really liked me. Liam liked her, and that tells you everything you need to know about the woman."

Jessica rolls her eyes. "Amongst other things."

As we walk down the hall to the kitchen, Jessica looks around her head nodding in appreciation. "I like what you've done with the place. It actually feels like a home. I've always hated Whitegates, but with Liam dead, this place has been given its souls back."

"We had a lot of fun doing it, didn't we, Chrissie?"

"Yeah, there was a lot of pleasure gained from selling all those stuffy antiques."

The past is the past, and the main thing is that we are all together again. My babies stir in my belly. They might never have a daddy, but they will grow up in a home full of love.

I try not to think about Simon and Imogen, but it's difficult, and I wonder if my family will ever be complete.

Taking a deep breath, I shake the sadness off and remind myself that this is a celebration, and I won't let my sorrow spoil it. I have to be grateful for what I have. Compared to where I was a few months back.

Chapter Twenty-Six

SIMON

The wind tugs at my jacket while the rain bites at my face. Daylight hours are reduced as winter advances, and mornings feel like the middle of the night. Today will be one of those dark, miserable days where the sun never makes it out. I try to shake off the fact that the weather seems to match my mood.

Turning, I walk down Front Street towards the house, having dropped Imogen off at school. My hands are buried deep in the pockets of my jacket as my fingers play with the house key.

Inside, the house looks the same as it always has. It amazes me how some things have stayed the same, never altered. Chrissie has gone, and yet everything remains just as it was the day she left. It is only when I look past the visual aspect that I feel the change. The house echoes with happy memories of a time now lost, never to return. It has taken me a long time to come to this conclusion, and it hurts every time I think about never seeing her again.

Life needs order, and I know I have to move on without Chrissie. Today is the day I begin, no matter how hard it is going to be.

Shaking out of my jacket and hanging it on the radiator to dry, I make myself a promise to start packing away Chrissie's things.

It has been over a year since she went missing, and I still have difficulty acknowledging that she is no longer here. I can't hide behind *maybe* anymore. I have to face the fact she is no longer a part of our lives, that she is never coming home.

The house smells of her. The walls, if I listen, resonate with her laughter. But that's all they are now, just memories, and they are ripping me apart. I have to move on, like Chrissie has moved on.

No one seems to know what has happened to her. There is no money trail, there have been no sightings, and there's no evidence to suggest that Chrissie has been abducted, or that something even more sinister has occurred. The police have no answers, just statistics on how frequently these types of things happen.

A lot of people left in my situation feel the same. They're certain that their loved ones would not just get up one day and walk out the door, disappearing from their lives without a reason. Her disappearance makes no sense. Still, I can't help clinging to the hope that, for whatever reason, she left to make a new life for herself. I can't stand the thought of someone taking her, of such a beautiful life ending.

No, it is easier to think she has left for something better, something I haven't been able to give her, no matter how much the thought hurts.

I sigh as I remove my soggy trainers and walk into the kitchen. The damp hem of my blue jeans brush against my socks as I walk. Switching the kettle on, I start making myself a coffee before doing anything else. I am aware that I am procrastinating, something Chrissie would say I excel at.

As the kettle boils, my thoughts turn to Imogen. This last year has been even worse for her than for me. She has grown up so quick since Chrissie's disappearance. Imogen blames herself, as children do. She can't understand why her mummy left, so her childish logic tells her it is her fault. I have no answers for her, other than to reassure her that Mummy's disappearance has nothing to do with her. I tell her both Mummy and Daddy love her very much. She mustn't blame herself.

The doorbell rings, pulling me from my melancholy.

Opening the front door, I stare at the woman before me. My heart hammers in my chest as I look at her. I know it isn't Chrissie, but she looks so familiar and so like Chrissie that my heart squeezes in pain.

"Hi." She sounds uncertain, a little scared even.

I take a slow, deep breath and steady my rambling brain.

"You must be Chrissie's sister." That can be the only explanation for the woman who looks so much like my wife.

"Yes." She hesitates. "I was wondering if I could talk to you."

I swing the door open. "Of course, come in."

"Sorry, I know this must be a bit of a shock for you."

"It's OK." I close the door and we head towards the kitchen. "I've just put the kettle on. Would you like a coffee or anything?"

The rubber soles of her trainers squeak on the oak flooring in the hall as she follows me.

"Coffee would be nice."

Without thinking, I reach for two mugs and begin making us a drink. Heating up the milk in the microwave as the kettle re-boils, I add the coffee, topping it up with water. It isn't until I turn to hand over the coffee that I realise what I have done. I have made the coffee for Chrissie.

"It's OK, we drink our coffee the same." She takes the mug from me. "Shall we sit down? I have a lot to tell you, and, to be honest, I'm not quite sure where to start."

I stand there, not moving. My heart is hammering and, while I don't want to ask, I need to know. "Is she alive?"

"Yes."

Thank God. Relief washes over me.

She watches me as I try to gather myself.

Finally, I find that I can move, and my heart begins returning to its natural rhythm. Pulling out a chair from the pine table, I sit down.

She shakes out of her coat, and I realize I am not being a good host.

"Sorry, I should have taken that." I stand up, reaching for it.

"Don't worry. I'll just drape it over the chair. It's horrid out there."

Her hair, so like Chrissie's, falls past her waist like spun silk. Though I know they are twins, it's hard for me to look at her and not see Chrissie. I feel the loss of my wife more now than I have ever felt it before. It is incredible how alike they are.

I stare at her unable to stop as I note the slight differences between them. Their eyes may have the same almond shape and tilt to them, and the colour is identical, but her eyes are softer. They don't have the same spark of confidence as

Chrissie's.

She fidgets, and I become conscious of how much I'm staring.

"Sorry."

"Don't worry. People used to stare at us all the time when we were kids. It was like one of those spot-the-difference games." Her hands curl round the mug as she talks.

"That must have been annoying." I say, conscious I am guilty doing the same thing.

"Sometimes, but we always got our own back – changing our name badges at school and pretending to be each other in class."

Silence falls, and the only noise is the rain against the kitchen window.

"I'm sorry to upset you. I know it has to be difficult, my being here, but I wanted you to know it wasn't Chrissie's fault. She never wanted to leave you."

She hesitates as she tries to find the right words… if they even exist. "I was married to a man who, well, was very controlling, powerful, and cruel. I was so unhappy, and I wanted out. There was no way he was going to let me leave, so I pretended to have cancer."

My shock must register on my face because she looks guilt stricken at what she has just confessed.

"It was the only way. If I had an illness that couldn't be cured, then there was nothing Liam could do about it. So, I changed my name to Jessica Ripley and moved to Scotland, starting a new life."

She takes a nervous sip of her coffee. "You have to understand that it never occurred to me that Liam would find out about Chrissie. I didn't even know you lived so close. But Liam did find out, and he took Chrissie and made her his. The fact she had amnesia from a fall, caused by a mugging, helped Liam gain the control over her he needed.

"Trust me, I would *never* have left if I thought he would take Chrissie away from you." Tears fill her eyes, and I watch in silence as she regains control.

"By the time Chrissie's memory came back, it was too late. Liam had integrated her into his life. He threatened to have you and Imogen killed if she said anything to anyone. She had no choice but to stay. You have to understand that."

The world I live in is simple. People like Liam don't exist in it. I could blame her for what has happened, tell her there is always a way out if you are strong enough, but I haven't lived her life, gone through what she has, so I don't know. My face tightens as my anger builds towards a man I have never met.

"Liam died at the end of summer. When I saw Chrissie's picture in the newspaper, I came back to York." Jessica wipes at her tears as she speaks. More take their place.

I can't remember seeing a photo of Chrissie in the paper, but then, high society and I are not friends, so I wouldn't have been interested.

Still, I don't understand. If this man is dead, why hasn't Chrissie come home? Did she think I wouldn't understand? Or that I would have simply moved on without her, that I no longer love her?

These are hard questions for me to face, but I have to ask. "Why has she not come home? Why stay away? The man's dead, she could have come home at any time."

Jessica looks uncomfortable. "It wasn't that easy for her."

"I don't understand." To me, it is that easy.

"Simon… Liam repeatedly raped her."

The chair scrapes against the tiles as I jump up from the

table and begin pacing. Violence has never been my way, yet I want nothing more than to pound my fists into this faceless man who not only took my wife from me but took Imogen's mummy. I feel sick, and my gut twists. Anger burns, and I feel as though I have let her down, let my family down.

"I don't understand why she won't come home. I'm angry, I'll admit. The thought of that man..." I can't say the word. "... Of what he did to her makes me furious. But I don't blame her, and I'll never stop loving her. She's my wife! Surely she knows that." Tears sting at the back of my eyes.

Jessica stands, taking a hesitant step forward. She touches my arm. "It's not you. She didn't come back because she was pregnant."

Bile rises in my throat and I swallow it down. Turning my back on Jessica, I stride over to the window, looking out at the falling rain. The garden is turning into a swimming pool, and I should get the pump out.

"I still love her," I whisper to the garden.

I hear footsteps behind me, and I turn to find Jessica sitting at the table, her hands wrapped around the cold mug of coffee. "She didn't want you to feel obligated to love another man's children. Chrissie had twins a couple of months ago."

Twins! I force myself to move away from the window, to sit at the table. "Twins?"

A shy smile falls across her lips. She nods. "Two boys."

Wow... My hands spread out on the wooden table. *Two boys... Wow.* When Chrissie became pregnant with Imogen, we laughed about the possibility of her having twins. She didn't, of course, but for her to have twins with this man... It stings, even though I know it shouldn't.

"Simon, I'm not here because I think you should know. I'm here because I don't want Chrissie to be sad anymore.

She's suffered because of me. Because I selfishly wanted to be happy. She doesn't know I'm here, and she'd have a fit if she did. I just wanted you to know. To give you the chance to see if you love her enough to accept her and the boys."

Loving Chrissie isn't the issue, it's the boys, the twins. My head is a mass of jumbled questions, resentment, and pain. This last year has been hell. Can I love another man's children, knowing how they were conceived? To be reminded of how that man raped my wife? And how I had been unable to prevent it.

I rub my temple, trying to ease the pounding in my head as the questions and my own indecision torment me.

"I'm not expecting an answer from you now. You've got a lot of thinking to do. But if you do decide that you want her, and the twins, this is where she's living now." She slides a small piece of paper towards me.

"I leave for Scotland tomorrow, and I couldn't leave without doing this. I hope you understand why." Standing, she picks up her coat. "I'll see myself out."

The paper sits on the table like a beacon. I don't hear the front door close behind her. Tears spill down my cheeks, and my hands shake as I close them over my face.

This isn't just about me. It's about Imogen as well. I can't destroy her world twice. I have to be sure I can accept the twins and be capable of loving them as though they are my own. I don't know if I can be strong enough to look at their tiny faces and not blame them in some way for what happened to Chrissie.

Sliding my hands from my face, I take a number of deep breaths. Loving Chrissie has always been so easy, and the twins are a part of her.

But…

KATHLEEN HARRYMAN

And that, right there, is the problem – BUT…
I bury my head in my hands and sob.
I'm just not sure I can love them, and I hate myself for it.

Chapter Twenty-Seven

CHRISSIE

It is late October, and another cold snap holds Yorkshire in its icy grip. Snow falls outside as I sit on the living room floor, staring out the window. The weather reports are saying that this could be the coldest October in over sixty years. The information adds to my worry.

Jessica, Charles, and their twins are back in Scotland. Weather conditions are worsening there, and I am resigning myself to Christmas without them. They stayed here longer than planned and their journey home was more difficult because of the sudden change in weather. While I'm desperate to have them here for Christmas, I know they are safer at home in Scotland.

William's cries pull my attention from the window, and he gurgles as I smile down at him. Thomas flails his arms and legs, afraid that his brother is receiving more attention, and I laugh at them.

"Now then, you two, has Mummy been neglecting you? Bad Mummy." I tickle both their bellies and their bodies wiggle with happiness.

They have my skin tone and almond-shaped eyes, but the intense blue of their eyes is all Liam. It doesn't bother me, not as I thought it would. These two beautiful boys will never grow to be like Liam.

A father is more, a *lot* more, than biological makeup. I think about Simon, and how he dotes on Imogen. Simon is a father.

I kept the photographs of Simon and Imogen that Liam threw at me the day he threatened to have them killed. They sit, in silver frames, on the oak sideboard near the large inglenook fireplace. I often sit there at night when everyone has gone to bed and talk to them. I tell them about the twins, and how I hope Imogen is doing well at school, and that Simon is looking after himself.

Sniffing the air, 1 look down at the wiggling babies. "Wow, you two smell. Come, let's get you changed."

They giggle as I scoop them to me lifting them into my arms taking them upstairs to their bedroom. They are too young to sleep in their own room, so they have cots in mine. However, I like them to spend time in what will be their bedroom, so I change them and put them down for naps in here to get them used to it. I did this with Imogen.

The room is decorated in light greens and yellows. Lions, elephants, giraffes, and bears roam along the walls. It is a little boys' bedroom.

They're both dressed in baby grows. William's is blue-and-white striped, and Thomas' is blue with white stars. The boys might look the same, but they are unique, each a little person in their own right, just like their mummy and Auntie Jessica. People often dress identical twins in the same clothes, but, being a twin myself, I know that it's important to let everyone know they are their own person, and not a clone of other.

I change Thomas first, as he is the smelliest. I swear these two little monsters are already trying to compete with one another. My nose wrinkles as I remove the nappy, and Thomas laughs.

"Well, I'm glad that you think it's funny."

This earns me another giggle from the happy little chap whose nappy is now clean.

"Chrissie!" Jenny calls.

"In here."

Jenny's footsteps mark a hurried beat up the stairs.

I swap the babies over and start changing William.

Moments later, Jenny appears. Her cheeks are rosy, and her hair falls about her shoulders.

I arch a brow at her. "What's got you all flustered?"

"There's a man downstairs asking for you."

I laugh. "It's the repairman, come to look at the washing machine."

"Well, I wish all repairmen looked like this one. If I'd known he was going to be that gorgeous, I'd have made more of an effort."

I look at Jenny's blue jeans and makeup-free face. Her hair frames her face in soft waves. "At least you did your hair. It looks fabulous, by the way."

"You think?" She twirls round so I get a three-sixty look.

"Absolutely."

Placing William in his cot, I tickle his belly and kiss his forehead before moving on to do the same to Thomas.

"Do you fancy putting them down for me? I'll go see to the repair man."

"I'd put on something a little less comfy if I were you. You might regret not doing so. Did I mention he's gorgeous?"

I glance at my black yoga pants and red sweat top. My hair hangs down my back, unbound. "I'll risk it."

"Your loss." Jenny shrugs as she reaches for a book, making herself comfortable in the rocking chair. "Again, H-O-T!"

"H-O-T or not, I'm not interested."

"You know, if I didn't love Dennis, *I'd* have given him a go."

Shaking my head at her, I make my way downstairs. I head for the kitchen, thinking that is where Jenny would have taken him.

Walking through the kitchen door, I am surprised to find only Jake Junior in the room. He's sitting at the table, perusing some landscape drawings.

"Have you seen the repairman?"

"Nope, but Jake took a chap into the living room."

"Why would Jake take the repairman into the living room to mend the washing machine?"

Junior shrugs. "I don't know."

Curiosity draws my brows together as I leave the kitchen and walk back towards the living room. Pushing the door open, I catch Jake sitting in the high-backed chair near the fireplace. His snow-white hair sticks up at strange angles from wearing the hat clasped in his hands.

Brows furrowed in concern, Jake looks across at the man hidden by the door.

"Jake, is everything OK?"

As I walk into the room, Jake stands up. "You remember what I said, lad." His fingers squeeze my arm as he walks past. "I have landscape plans to go over before Jake Junior gets carried away. It's only a flower bed or two that we're replacing, not the whole damn garden." Jake shuffles to the door. "You know where I am if you need me."

I stand rooted to the spot, looking at the man on the sofa. His hair has grown to his shoulders, and a few extra lines have formed at the corners of his eyes. His mouth curves in a nervous smile and his hands remain clasped in his lap, resting on black jeans.

My eyes eat him up, and I wish I *had* changed, as Jenny suggested. I feel unprepared as I look at the gorgeous man who I never thought I would see again.

Love pours through me, and my heart doesn't seem to know if it should summersault with joy or beat harder with fear as my eyes lock onto Simon's.

"Simon?" His name falls from my lips. "How..."

He looks nervous. "Jessica came to see me."

"Ahhh." Fear prevents me from asking why he's here, because now that he *is* here, I don't ever want him to leave. If he's not going to stay, I don't want to know. Not yet.

"I've been doing a lot of thinking, Chrissie."

Judging by the shadows beneath his eyes, he has been doing more thinking than sleeping.

I brace myself, knowing that, even now, I can't make him stay. He needs to make his own choice, without any influence from me. "It's OK, Simon, I understand. You didn't need to come here to explain."

If Jessica had been to see Simon, she would have told him what happened to me. About Liam. About William and Thomas.

"Jessica's heart was in the right place, but really, I understand. I don't expect you to accept me and the boys."

Simon pushes himself off the sofa and, before I can say anything, he wraps his arms around me.

I cling on to him. Tears roll down both our faces.

"I love you so much, Chrissie, so much. This last year has been hell without you."

His lips touch my head, and I bury myself deeper in his chest, breathing him in.

As much as I want Simon, I have to face the truth. Unless he can accept and love William and Thomas, there is no way we can be together.

Scared of rejection, I realize that perhaps I didn't speak to Simon after Liam died because I was afraid to hear him tell me he couldn't accept my babies.

"I need to see the boys. I need to know that I can love them."

I nod, lifting my head from his chest.

"I'm sorry, Chrissie. I wish I could say that I don't need to know, to reassure myself… that… that…"

Resting my fingers against his lips, I silence him. "It's OK, Simon, I understand."

His arms tighten around me, and somehow, I find the strength I need to push out of his embrace, take his hand, and guide him upstairs for William and Thomas to work their magic.

"It's going to be OK."

Simon smiles at me as he wipes the tears from my face. "You were always the one with the faith. In all the time I've known you, somehow you have always made everything work."

Leaning down, he brushes his lips against mine as we stand on the landing. My breath catches as our lips met. Doubt crawls along my skin, and I promise myself I won't let either of us down. I have to remain confident on the outside despite the fear sitting in my stomach. Today isn't going to be any different.

"Come on." I give his hand a squeeze.

Jenny looks up from the rocking chair. The book she is reading sits in her lap. Placing a finger on her lips, she stands up. If she wonders why I am holding the repairman's hand, she doesn't say anything.

"Dennis and Elsie will be home soon. I'd better go down and start doing something for tea." As she walks out of the room, she kisses my cheek. "He'd be nuts to let you go," she whispers in my ear.

Closing my eyes, I call on all the strength I possess. I take Simon over to meet my boys. "This is Thomas, and this one is William," I say softly.

As if sensing that there is a stranger in their room, they both open their eyes and let out a cry.

"Shhh…" I whisper, tickling their bellies.

William and Thomas' cries continue, and I lean over to pick up Thomas. Balancing him against my chest, I turn to get William. His cot is empty, and I look over to find Simon holding him.

A contented gurgle comes from William's lips.

"Well, hello, little man."

William blows a happy bubble at Simon, who kisses his forehead.

Simon looks at me. "Wait until Imogen finds out she has two brothers to boss about."

I can't say anything, so I nod as tears run down my cheeks. I never thought I would be lucky enough to have Simon and Imogen back in my life.

"Come here." Simon reaches for me, and I step into his

waiting arms. "I've been a fool. I know that now. These little chaps are a part of you. How could I not love them?"

Simon isn't the only fool. I should have told him about Liam and the boys all those months ago when I sat outside our house waiting for him to come home. Instead, like a coward, I slunk away, never allowing him the chance to make up his own mind.

Simon's lips meet mine. "I love you so much, Chrissie."

My heart beats in the rhythm it has always drummed when Simon and I are together. I feel like it is welcoming him home.

I am whole again.

Miracles are funny things. Sometimes they take their time to mate-rialise, but once they do, they are worth every second, hour, day, week, month, or year that you waited for them to arrive. Because when they do show up, that feeling lasts a lifetime.

About the Author

Kathleen Harryman is a storyteller and poet living in the historically rich city of York, North Yorkshire, England, with her husband, children and pet dog and cat.

The Other Side of the Looking Glass was first published in 2015. Since then, Kathleen has developed a unique writing style which readers have enjoyed, and she became a multi-genre author of suspense, psychological thrillers, poetry, and historical romance.

**FOR MORE INFORMATION ABOUT
KATHLEEN HARRYMAN, VISIT:**

www.kathleenharryman.com

Connect on Twitter: @KathleenHarrym1

Printed in Poland
by Amazon Fulfillment
Poland Sp. z o.o., Wrocław